"How is that letter-writing service going?" Mr. Wakefield asked.

Elizabeth smiled tiredly and flopped down on the sofa. "Well, it's been incredibly lucrative, but Jessica and I both feel that the letter-writing business takes too much time away from the other things we have to do, like homework and seeing our friends. We know we need to slow down." Elizabeth folded her arms across her chest. "I'm just not sure *what* we're going to do."

Elizabeth picked up the U.S. Sports catalog and flipped automatically to the warmup jacket she had ordered for Todd. It was due to arrive any day now, and then she could finally tell him what had been keeping her so busy. But for some reason, Elizabeth felt melancholy. She glanced quickly at her parents, contentedly sharing an evening together just reading and talking, and she thought about how little she had seen Todd during the past weeks. Somehow, her plan didn't seem worth it anymore. "Right now," she said, surprising herself with the firmness of her tone, "I'm ready to quit altogether."

Bantam Books in the Sweet Valley High series
Ask your bookseller for the books you have missed

LOVE LETTERS
FOR SALE

Written by
Kate William

Created by
FRANCINE PASCAL

BANTAM BOOKS
NEW YORK • TORONTO • LONDON • SYDNEY • AUCKLAND

To Amy Ellen Dyson

RL 6, IL age 12 and up

LOVE LETTERS FOR SALE
A Bantam Book / October 1992

Sweet Valley High is a registered trademark of Francine Pascal

Conceived by Francine Pascal

Produced by Daniel Weiss Associates, Inc.
33 West 17th Street
New York, NY 10011

Cover art by James Mathewuse

ISBN 0-553-29234-X

Published simultaneously in the United States and Canada

Bantam Books are published by Bantam Books, a division of Bantam Doubleday Dell Publishing Group, Inc. Its trademark, consisting
of the words "Bantam Books" and the portrayal of a rooster, is
Registered in U.S. Patent and Trademark Office and in other coun-
tries. Marca Registrada. Bantam Books, 666 Fifth Avenue, New
York, New York 10103.

PRINTED IN THE UNITED STATES OF AMERICA

OPM   0 9 8 7 6 5 4 3 2 1

self busy dating almost every eligible guy at Sweet Valley High and beyond. But when Sam had ridden into her life on his motorcycle, his wavy blond hair tousled endearingly over his gray eyes, Jessica gave up her wandering ways. Well, almost. There had been times when she had strayed, like when she thought she had fallen for Brandon Hunter, the star of her favorite soap opera, *The Young and the Beautiful*.

But Brandon Hunter and Jessica's week of fame as a soap star were a thing of the past. At that moment, Jessica wasn't thinking about acting, other guys, or journalistic censorship. Sure, she was proud that Elizabeth had ignored the initial cautions of the school newspaper's advisor and the outright restrictions of Sweet Valley High's principal and printed her article on harassment anyway. But right now, Jessica was thinking about something much more important—money. Or rather, the lack of it.

Jessica sipped her soda and snuggled closer to Sam. She smiled and kissed him on the cheek.

"What was that for?" Sam asked, his eyes twinkling.

"Just because," Jessica teased. "Do I have to have a reason?"

Sam shook his head and grinned. "No way! Feel free, anytime."

Free. Sam's comment had made her think about money again! If only that sleek new compact disc player that she had seen at Stereo City were free. Jessica had spotted the portable player at the mall when she and her best friends, Lila Fowler and

Amy Sutton, were shopping the night before and she hadn't been able to stop thinking about it. Especially since she had put it on layaway. Jessica liked layaways. The trouble was, she now had both a dress at Lisette's *and* the CD player waiting for her. Though the sale prices on the items were locked in, she still didn't have the money to buy them. She wasn't even sure she would have the money in a month, when the layaway time ran out.

The seventeen dollars she now had left in her savings account wasn't even going to come *close*, and next month's allowance was already advanced and spent. Sam's birthday was coming up, and she wanted to buy him a new pair of gloves to wear when he was racing his dirt bike. And Jessica had been toying with the idea of redecorating her room. She was *tired* of Hershey Bar brown!

Jessica sighed. This was just another example of the difference between herself and Elizabeth. Jessica had no money and no idea what she wanted to be when she grew up. Elizabeth, on the other hand, not only had her life and future career as a writer plotted out, she also had her finances well in hand. Jessica couldn't remember her sister ever needing an advance on her allowance. And when Elizabeth *did* come into an extra sum of money, she either put it in the bank or spent it on something practical.

Jessica sighed again. She needed to come up with a new money-making idea, and fast!

"I think I'm going to start a business," Jessica announced suddenly.

"Doing what?" Sam asked.

"I don't know. Got any ideas? I'm in dire straits, moneywise."

"What happened to all the money you and Elizabeth made working on the soap opera?" Todd asked.

"Oh, it wasn't that much," Jessica said. "Not as much as we thought it would be, anyway. We spent most of it helping to pay for the Jeep."

"Don't forget the clothes you bought, and those new CDs, and going out to dinner, and . . ." Elizabeth teased.

"You don't have any of your share left, either," Jessica retorted good-naturedly.

"But I do have something to show for it—my new computer and word-processing program," Elizabeth said. "It makes writing for *The Oracle* much less time-consuming. Now I don't have to start over every time I make a mistake. I just edit on the screen and print a perfect page. I love it!"

"You're so easily pleased," Jessica joked. "As for me, I need a little more adventure in my life than writing the perfect page."

"We're still recovering from your last adventure with Club X," Sam reminded her. "Do you think you could give your loved ones at least a week of peace and quiet?"

"Sure," Jessica said, laughing. "I said I needed a *job*, not an adventure."

The conversation turned back to Elizabeth's victory in the world of journalism, and Jessica let her attention drift to the conversation going on next to her. Jessica and Elizabeth had invited a few friends to their house for an informal get-together. It was great to kick back and relax. That's why Jessica was so surprised when Lila got up to leave.

"You're not leaving so early, are you?" Amy Sutton asked Lila as she stood up.

"Stuff to do," Lila commented offhandedly. "Nothing I'm thrilled about doing, that's for sure."

"Homework?"

"No way. I wouldn't let homework keep me from socializing," Lila declared.

That's typical, Jessica thought. Lila Fowler was one of the richest and most popular girls in town, and she *never* let schoolwork interfere with her social life. Come to think of it, neither did Jessica.

"No," Lila continued. "I have to write a letter to this dippy cousin of mine in New York. I've been putting it off for weeks. We don't have a thing in common, and we're barely on speaking terms, but our parents insist that we correspond for the sake of the family."

"How dull," Amy said. "That's almost as bad as the letter I've been putting off writing."

Jessica leaned closer, the glimmer of an idea beginning to form in her mind. "What's yours about?" she asked.

"My great-aunt knitted me a ridiculous orange-and-green sweater for my birthday, and I have to write her a thank-you letter. The trouble is, it's

6

hard to be sincere about something that makes me look like the Great Pumpkin. I wish I could talk someone into writing the letter for me. I'd even pay them!"

"Me, too," Lila said. "Writing to Cousin Pete is a huge waste of my time. I'd gladly pay someone else to write the letters."

"I might as well go, too," Amy said, standing up.

"Need a lift?" Lila asked. "Hey, I have an idea. Why don't you come over to my house? We can commiserate about writing those letters."

Jessica raised one eyebrow thoughtfully as Lila and Amy left. Maybe this was it, the idea she had been hoping for. A letter-writing service! Why hadn't she thought of it before? If Amy and Lila hated writing letters and were willing to pay someone to do it for them, there must be dozens of others like them who would also pay.

How much could she charge for letters? she wondered. Three, four, five dollars? At that rate, how many letters would it take to buy the CD player for the Jeep and the gloves for Sam? Quick calculations told her that the letter-writing service was a *great* idea!

There was only one tiny, little problem. Jessica didn't like to write letters any more than the next person. In fact, unless it was an occasional humorous piece for *The Oracle*, Jessica didn't like to write at all. She glanced over at Elizabeth, who was still extolling the virtues of her new word processor.

But she knew someone who did.

*　　*　　*

Elizabeth noticed Jessica's calculating look but decided to ignore it. Jessica was always planning some scheme and sooner or later she would tell her sister. That was the way it had always been between the twins. Though they had identical features, their personalities were as different as night and day. Elizabeth was the steady one; Jessica had flighty written all over her.

But when it came to support, Elizabeth and Jessica were always there for each other, and they had each done their share of pulling the other out of a scrape or two—or three. That's why Elizabeth knew Jessica wouldn't keep her in the dark for long about the idea that was clearly hatching in her fertile imagination.

Right now, though, Elizabeth was more concerned about Shelley Novak. Shelley and her boyfriend, Jim Roberts, had just arrived at the Wakefields', and Shelley looked distracted.

"So, how's the girls' basketball team shaping up?" Elizabeth asked when Shelley and Jim joined the group. "I was watching you at practice last week, and your offensive line looks fantastic."

"Thanks," Shelley said, smiling.

"So, are you ready for the first state championship playoff game this weekend?" Elizabeth asked.

"I hope so! Coach Tilman is counting on us. And he's working us pretty hard, too. We still need to play more as a team instead of as a bunch of individual players. The coach is drilling pass maneuvers into us for hours a day!"

8

Jessica laughed. "That doesn't leave much time for a social life."

Shelley's smile slipped for a split second. "Not really, but we try our best, don't we, Jim?"

Jim nodded. "The only way I get to see her anymore is to show up at practices and games."

"Have you finished all the photos for the yearbook yet?" Todd asked.

"No. And I've been spending so much time in the darkroom lately, I've begun to think I'm a creature of the night," Jim said.

Everybody laughed. Except Shelley, Elizabeth noticed.

"Hey, congratulations on your harassment article," Shelley said, changing the subject. "The whole school is still buzzing about it. Do you think the administration will let you have more control over what goes into the paper now?"

"Definitely," Elizabeth replied. "But I don't have any new controversial articles planned, if that's what you mean!"

Shelley frowned. "I have an idea for you. How about student athletes on drugs? Remember what happened to Tony Esteban? Annie Whitman told me the other day that since he got clean, he's been giving a lot of talks at junior high schools, trying to discourage kids from taking steroids and other drugs to build themselves up. According to Tony, the problem is getting worse."

Jessica nodded thoughtfully. "I talked to Annie the other day, too," she said. "She told me that Tony is so tied up with giving talks that she hardly sees him anymore. She said that if she didn't know better, she would think he was seeing someone else!"

There was an awkward silence. Elizabeth noted Shelley's flushed face and Jim's fingers nervously tapping his leg. She decided to follow Shelley's example of a moment before and change the subject.

"There must be a huge need for kids to hear horror stories from someone who knows about drugs firsthand," she said. "Maybe we do need an article in the paper. You know, Olivia Davidson was talking about a poem on drug abuse someone submitted for *Visions*, her literary magazine. It doesn't hurt to remind people about important issues every few months or so. What do you think, Jess?"

Jessica grinned. "I think you're the best writer around, Liz. If anyone can do an article on such a sensitive subject, you can. In fact, I'm sure you could write just about anything someone asked you to write."

"Thanks," Elizabeth said, taken slightly aback. Usually when Jessica came out with a big compliment like that, she was trying to butter someone up. Elizabeth took a sip of her soda and chewed on a piece of ice, waiting for Jessica to reveal what was really on her mind, but Jessica didn't oblige her. Instead, she turned to Sam and started talking about the dirt bike race he was going to be in the following weekend.

"So what are your plans for tonight, the last night before the first playoff game?" Todd asked Shelley and Jim.

Jim looked at his watch. "Uh-oh. I'd better get going," he said, standing up. "In fact, I only meant to stop by and say hello. I have a ton of enlargements to make tonight and a report to finish for World History."

"It's a shame when schoolwork interferes with your photography, isn't it?" Todd joked.

Jim shook his head forlornly. "Yeah," he agreed. "Don't these teachers realize that we have better things to do with our time than study?"

As Jim stood up to leave Shelley put her hand on his arm. "I thought we were going to go out together later tonight," she said softly, biting her bottom lip.

"Gosh, I'm sorry, Shel," Jim said. "I'm so swamped that I doubt I'll get any sleep as it is. Want me to give you a ride home?"

"Sure," Shelley said, her shoulders slumped.

Elizabeth watched the couple as they headed for the front door. Shelley was definitely dragging her feet, and Elizabeth wondered whether there was more to her friend's mood than one broken date.

"Something is wrong with Shelley," she whispered to Todd. "She seemed really uncomfortable tonight. Why don't you try to catch her at basketball practice tomorrow and see if she'll talk to you?"

"OK," Todd said, glancing after the couple. "But it looks as if they're just experiencing the time crunch, like everyone else. There simply aren't enough hours in the day for some of us."

"That's for sure," Jessica added. "Between

11

school and cheerleading practice and a dozen other activities, I don't know when I'm going to find time to start a business."

"OK, Jess. Talk!" Elizabeth said when their friends had all gone home and they were alone. "You've been hinting around about something all night."

Jessica knew it was time to launch into her sales pitch. "Well," she began, "you know I've been thinking about getting a job to make a little extra spending money . . ."

"Yes. So?"

"While everyone was here earlier, I had an idea. What about a letter-writing service?" Jessica paused for a quick breath. "I heard Lila and Amy talking about how they had to write letters to relatives and how they would *gladly* pay someone else to do it for them, and I thought if Amy and Lila were willing to pay, then there must be dozens of others out there who hate writing letters, too.

"Anyway, I thought we could advertise and offer to write the letters for those people for a fee—and we would make them happy, save them time, and make a quick profit in the process."

Elizabeth smiled. "It sounds like a great idea."

"Look, I know you think this is just another one of my hare-brained schemes," Jessica raced on, "but I've thought about this seriously. I think it could really work. We could get a post office box so no one knows who's behind the service, because we might want to be anonymous, you know. And we could put up posters all over town

12

and at school. Isn't there anything you'd like to buy with some extra money?"

Elizabeth laughed. "Jessica, if you would stop talking for a minute and listen, you'd realize that I said I think your idea is a good one," she teased. "You're so busy trying to convince me, you didn't even hear me say yes!"

Jessica stared at Elizabeth. "You did?"

Elizabeth giggled. "I did."

"But why?"

"You're crazy, Jess," Elizabeth said. "A minute ago you were trying to sell me your plan, and now you're asking me *why* I like it, as if you're hoping I'll say no."

"I can't help it," Jessica said, joining in Elizabeth's laughter. "I'm just used to having to fight a battle."

"I'm not *that* bad."

"Sometimes you are."

"Not this time. A letter-writing service might just make me the extra money I need right now, too. I saw a great warmup jacket in the U.S. Sports catalog that would look perfect on Todd. I promised myself that I would do something special for him because he's always doing great things for me. But the jacket costs a hundred dollars."

"You're beginning to sound like me," Jessica said. "I put a CD player for the Jeep on layaway at Stereo City."

"Well, then, I guess we'll have to work together to earn the money," Elizabeth said.

"I'll get a notepad," Jessica said, rummaging

13

through her backpack, "and we'll start right now."

Elizabeth grinned. "Who's the organized one around here?" she asked with mock indignation. "Now *you* sound like *me!*"

Two

"Shelley's game seems a little off today," Elizabeth commented to Todd when he joined her on the bleachers during a break in practice Friday afternoon. "She's usually a whiz at rebounding, but she's missed two easy lay-ups in the past five minutes."

Todd wiped his forehead with his towel and looked out to the court where the girls' team was practicing. Both Sweet Valley High's basketball teams were top-ranked. The winning record of the girls' team was due largely to Shelley Novak, who was famous for her high-scoring games. In fact, Shelley had recently won a $5,000 scholarship as the Varsity Club Athlete of the Year. As usual, both teams were practicing at the same time—on opposite ends of the court—after school. Sometimes they even played a scrimmage against each other.

"You're right," Todd said after observing Shelley's stilted actions on the court. "Her timing is off. She must have something on her mind. I hope she'll work through it before the game tonight."

"It's going to be quite an evening—the first playoff game for the state championship. I'm sorry I'm going to miss it," Elizabeth said.

"Me, too. But say hi to Steven for me."

"I will. We're going to meet him in San Farando and take him out to dinner at Pedro's," Elizabeth told him.

Todd ruffled her hair. "The Wakefield rescue squad."

"Well, Steven *has* been a little depressed since Cara moved to England. Every so often we try to get him to take a break from the books, cheer him up a little."

"I wish you could be here cheering on the girls' team with me," Todd said.

"Me, too. I'll be thinking about them, though. And you." Elizabeth kissed him. "You taste salty," she said.

"Yum," Todd teased. "I'd better get back out there. Break time is over."

"I can't stay much longer, but I'm going to try to talk to Shelley before I go."

"Good idea," Todd agreed as he bounded down off the bleachers.

The girls' team took a break then, and Shelley wandered past Elizabeth, her water bottle tilted up to spray her face.

"Shelley!" Elizabeth called, patting the bench next to her. "Got a minute?"

16

"Sure," Shelley said, sitting down next to Elizabeth. "I'm exhausted!"

Maybe that's it, Elizabeth thought. *Shelley's just tired.* "What have you been doing lately?" Elizabeth asked. "And where's Jim? I didn't notice him hanging around practice today."

Shelley frowned. "I don't have any idea where Jim is," she said, somewhat testily.

"What's wrong, Shelley?" Elizabeth asked. "You've seemed kind of down lately."

Shelley's frown turned into a sad smile, her almond-shaped brown eyes holding Elizabeth's for a long moment. "Nothing specific," she said, turning away to stare out across the gymnasium floor. "Do you know that I grew another half-inch last month?"

"No, I didn't. Is that good or bad?"

"Good, I suppose. It puts me just that much closer to the basket."

"You're not worried again about being too tall, are you?" Elizabeth asked gently. It hadn't been that long since Shelley had learned to like herself the way she was. Until Jim had come along, Shelley had been convinced that she wasn't pretty enough or special enough to keep a guy interested. Jim had convinced her that she was unique and fascinating, not to mention beautiful, and the change in Shelley's attitude had been phenomenal.

"No," Shelley said, answering Elizabeth's question. "I thought at first that maybe that was what was bugging me, but then I realized that my height is the least of my problems." She smiled

17

ruefully. "I appreciate your concern, Liz, but there's nothing you can do."

"Well, if you ever need a friendly shoulder . . ." Elizabeth offered.

"Thanks. I'll remember that."

"Good luck at the game tonight," Elizabeth said as Shelley hopped down and ran back out to the court.

Shelley gave her a thumbs-up sign as Elizabeth wondered again what it was that was bothering her. She watched the tandem practices for a few more minutes, then gathered her backpack and climbed down off the bleachers.

Elizabeth hailed Todd from the sidelines, and he jogged over to her while the rest of the team practiced lay-ups in two long lines stretching to center court.

"I'll see you tomorrow," Elizabeth said, kissing him goodbye. "I'll be thinking about you tonight while I'm eating Mexican food."

Todd smiled. "Have a few nachos for me."

"I will. Listen, I talked to Shelley, but she won't tell me what's wrong. If you get a chance, try to talk to her after practice today. I kind of suspect some of her old insecurities are cropping up. Remember when she first met Jim and wasn't sure anyone could like her? She thought she was too tall, and not pretty, and that boys were put off by her talent in basketball."

"Not Jim," Todd reminded her.

"I know. Jim helped her gain confidence in herself, but he's been awfully busy lately and Shelley seems depressed."

18

"What about Cathy Ulrich? She's Shelley's best friend," Todd asked.

"I didn't see Cathy out on the court today," Elizabeth said. "I hope Shelley's mood doesn't affect her game tonight."

"Don't worry, Liz. I'm sure she'll be fine," Todd said. "I'll talk to her, though, if you want."

"Thanks," Elizabeth told him. "See you tomorrow."

"What a practice!" Todd exclaimed as he sat down on the bench next to Shelley thirty minutes later. "I hope I have enough energy for the game later."

Shelley shook her head. "*You* only have to watch. *I* have to play. I know Coach thinks a good workout before a game revs up our engines, but lately I'm not so sure," she said. "I'll need a solid twelve-course dinner just to get my motor to turn over."

Todd laughed. "Not twelve courses! Coach Tilman would have a fit! 'Eat light,' he always says. 'Eat light and fly!'"

"More likely blow away," Shelley joked. "I can see it now. All of a sudden, in the middle of a game, all of the players start floating off into space." The image made her smile, and she forgot for a moment the problems she was having with Jim.

"Hey, that's better," Todd said. "I haven't seen you smile all afternoon. Is the coach on your case, or what?"

Shelley looked into Todd's liquid brown eyes

19

and suddenly knew she could tell him what was on her mind. He was so easy to talk to. And he really listened. Not like Jim. Jim was so wrapped up in his photography that he rarely heard a word she said.

"No," she began, staring at her clasped hands. "The coach isn't on my case. It's Jim. He's been so distracted lately. I know he's busy with the yearbook photos and other stuff, but we hardly see each other anymore and, well, I'm beginning to wonder if it's something I've done."

She looked up at Todd's concerned expression and suddenly wished she could take back her words. She didn't want his pity. She squared her shoulders. "Never mind," she told him. "Forget I said that. We'll work it out."

"Don't worry, Shelley. I won't say anything to Jim. But if you want my opinion, I don't think it's anything you've done. You're a nice person, a good friend, a great basketball player. Jim's lucky to have you as his girlfriend."

Shelley drank in Todd's much-needed praise. "Thanks," she said. "I wish Jim and I could talk so easily. It seems that every time I bring up the subject of our relationship, he zones out. He nods his head and says 'uh-huh,' but he's really off in outer space somewhere."

Todd grinned. "Guys are like that sometimes, Shelley. Remember when I got obsessed about the fraternity rushes? I had only one thing on my mind: get *my* pledges accepted and Bruce Patman's rejected. I ignored everyone, even Liz. She practically had to conk me over the head before I noticed that the rest of the world was going by without me. That's probably what's happening to Jim with the yearbook deadline looming so close."

"Probably," Shelley said slowly, wanting to believe that Todd was right and that she was just imagining Jim's indifference.

"Listen, I've got to go home and get something to eat before the game tonight," Todd said. "Cheer up!"

"OK," Shelley said with an attempt at a smile. "See you later."

Shelley sat on the bench for a long while after Todd left. Elizabeth was so lucky. Todd was so easy to talk to, so sincere, so genuine. She didn't really remember what had happened between Bruce and Todd, but she doubted that Todd was ever so obsessed with anything that he neglected Elizabeth the way Jim was neglecting her. Still, it was nice of Todd to try to cheer her up.

She *did* feel better after having talked to him, better than she had the whole past week. Maybe Todd *was* right. Maybe Jim was just really busy and didn't notice that she was feeling left out of his life. If that was true, there was still a future for them.

Shelley was still feeling lighthearted that night at the game. She played extremely well, scoring sixteen points in the first half alone. When the coach called a timeout with two minutes left in the game, she ran over to the sidelines with her teammates.

Shelley glanced up into the stands at Todd.

Much to her surprise she had heard him calling her name, cheering her on. She knew she was playing better that night than she had that afternoon because he was watching her. It was almost as good as having Jim in the crowd.

"OK, girls," Coach Tilman said. "We're down by five points and we're going to make that up in the next two minutes. Right?"

"*Right!*" the girls shouted.

"Shelley, I want you right up under the basket. We're counting on you."

"Yes, Coach," she answered.

"All right. Let's do it!" Coach Tilman ordered.

"Go, Shelley!" she heard Todd shout.

Adrenaline rushed through Shelley as the other team tossed in the ball. She stole it from their center, passed it to Cathy, and headed for the basket to set up the shot. Cathy passed it to Emily, and Emily backhanded it to Shelley for the layup.

The crowd went wild. "Novak, Novak, Novak!" they chanted when they weren't shouting "Sweet Valley, Sweet Valley." Shelley didn't have to look to know that Todd was leading the chant.

The Sacramento team's forward tossed in the ball to the point guard and Cathy immediately zeroed in, peeling the ball away from the guard before she had a chance to notice. A sense of power surged through Shelley as she watched her friend unsuccessfully try to breach the other team's defenses. Cathy shot from the top of the key and sunk it as the gymnasium shook with the sound of stomping feet.

One point down and only thirty seconds left. They were so close. They couldn't let the other team run out the clock. With a burst of speed, Shelley charged and intercepted a pass, forcing the turnover they badly needed. She headed downcourt, eyes fixed on the basket, dodging the bodies in her way. She leaped as the clock ticked down to two seconds, one second . . . she threw the ball . . . it hit the rim as the buzzer sounded, rolling around with agonizing slowness.

The crowd held its collective breath and then exploded in a deafening roar as the ball fell through the net, winning the game.

She had done it. Shelley Novak was the hero of the first playoff game. They were one step closer to the state championship. Suddenly, everyone was hugging her and swinging her around.

Cathy slapped her on the back. "Great shot, Shelley," she said. "Why use basketball shoes when you have wings?"

"All in a day's work," Shelley said, grinning and slapping her friend in turn.

Shelley looked up to see Todd coming toward her. "Great game. Congratulations, Shelley!" he said.

"Thanks." She wanted to tell him she owed it all to him, to his willingness to listen when she was down earlier that afternoon, but she was caught up in the frenzied celebration of her teammates. "See you," was all she managed to say.

But even as Shelley allowed herself to be dragged into the screaming, jumping, shouting mass of people on the court, she was thinking about Todd Wilkins. She wondered what it would be like to be Elizabeth Wakefield and have a guy like Todd around all of the time. She bet it would be nice.

"So, how is life in Sweet Valley?" Steven asked when the Wakefield family had all settled into a booth at Pedro's. The Mexican restaurant was their favorite place to eat in San Farando, a town that was halfway between Sweet Valley and the state college, where Steven was a prelaw student, like his father had been.

Jessica was studying her menu, so Elizabeth answered. "The same—school, homework, parties."

"I heard you shook things up at school recently," Steven said. "Dad told me that you bucked the system."

"I did, but that's not unusual for a Wakefield, is it? We live for excitement."

"That sounds like something Jess would say, not you, Liz," Steven teased. "Maybe you two are more alike than anyone realizes."

"Just two peas in a pod," Jessica quipped. "Seriously, though, we're going to put some of our combined talents to good use. Elizabeth and I are going into business together."

"Ah, so the idea of making money with a business of your own has finally jelled. A partnership sounds good," Mr. Wakefield remarked. "What kind of business is it? Do you need an attorney? I know where you can find one of the best, you know," he teased.

Elizabeth laughed. "Thanks, but no thanks, Dad. We're starting a letter-writing service," she told him. "We're going to offer to write letters for people, for a fee. We've already rented a post office box and made up flyers."

"Not a bad idea," Mrs. Wakefield said. "There've been times when I've wished I had someone to write a few letters for me. I might be calling on your services. Are you sure you don't need someone to design your office for you? We could work a trade."

"You're not touching my room," Jessica remarked lightly. "I like it just the way it is."

Mrs. Wakefield threw up her hands in surrender. "If you want chocolate-brown walls and the Early American Clutter style, that's fine with me. Just continue to keep your door shut when company comes over. I want to keep my clients."

"I don't think you have to worry, Mom," Elizabeth reassured her. "Besides, we're going to base our operations out of *my* room, where the all-essential computer is located."

"Good plan," Mr. Wakefield said, giving Jessica's ear a playful tug. "At least we'll be able to find the office to do the books come tax time."

"How much are you going to charge per letter?" Steven wanted to know.

Jessica smiled and rubbed her hands together. "Five dollars per letter, which will include postage to mail our letter back to the sender. That way the sender can either just sign the typed letter that Elizabeth prints out on her computer, or they can copy it over in their own handwriting."

"I'll bet there are a few people in the dorm who would be interested in your service," Steven mused. "Do you have any of your flyers with you?"

"I was hoping you'd ask," Jessica said, digging in her bag. "I just happen to have twenty right here."

Everyone laughed.

"I can see who's the public-relations end of this business," Mr. Wakefield commented as he took one of the flyers to read. "A-ha! Good for you. It's always smart to include a little legal disclaimer."

"Read it aloud, Ned," Mrs. Wakefield encouraged.

" 'Letters R Us,' " the twins' father began reading. " 'Do you have a letter to write that's giving you a headache? Let Letters R Us write your letter for you. Personal or business—no problem too large, no letter impossible to write.' And my favorite part is here at the bottom," Mr. Wakefield continued. " 'Letters R Us claims no responsibility for the reaction of anyone receiving a letter written by us.' "

"Your flyer is good," Steven said. "Short and to the point."

"Just don't go overboard and take on so many clients that the business interferes with your schoolwork," Mr. Wakefield cautioned.

"We won't, Dad," Elizabeth was quick to reassure him. "It's going to be a short-term business, anyway, just until we reach our financial goals."

"Yeah," Jessica added. "Just until we make millions!"

26

Three

Jessica was thrilled. It was only Tuesday and already there were four requests for letters in their new post office box. She and Elizabeth had put the flyers up just the Friday before. The plan was that Jessica would drop off and pick up the mail, and open and sort the requests. Elizabeth would do most of the actual writing of the letters, but the girls would consult on any difficult issues that might come up.

Not that Jessica expected to receive many requests for difficult letters. She figured that most of the requests they received would be for letters similar to the ones that Amy and Lila had had to write the week before. She scanned the return addresses on the envelopes in her hand. Wouldn't it be ironic, she thought, if one of their first requests was from Lila or Amy, the two people without whom Jessica would never have come up

27

with the idea in the first place? Of course, she could never tell them that she and Elizabeth were the brains behind the operation, because to reveal the identities of the people behind Letters R Us would ruin their chances of receiving requests from people at Sweet Valley High. Jessica wasn't exactly sure *why*, but a lot of people seemed to have the idea that she couldn't keep a secret.

"Look at this, Liz!" she called as she entered their house a few minutes later and raced up the stairs to her sister's room. She waved the letters in front of Elizabeth's astonished face. "We already have four requests. That's twenty dollars!"

"Let's see," Elizabeth said excitedly as she stored the document she had been writing on her computer and joined Jessica on the bed.

Jessica ripped open the first envelope.

" 'To whom it may concern,' " Jessica read. " 'My neighbor stole my cat. Talking hasn't worked. Will you please write a letter to her explaining that I want my Fluffy back and that I'm prepared to go to the authorities if necessary? Enclosed is five dollars. I hope you can help me.' "

"The poor woman. She sounds so distraught," Elizabeth said. "I'll write a nice, but firm letter to her rotten neighbor. What kind of person would want to abduct someone's cat?"

"You have to be kidding," Jessica said. "*Any* kind of person. I can think of a million reasons why someone would want to get rid of a neighbor's cat. I mean, what if the cat is going—you know—in their flower beds? Or wailing at night? Or fighting with *their* cat?"

"OK, I get your point. But the request is from the cat's *owner*, so we have to write the letter *she* asked for."

"I can't believe it," Jessica snorted. "A stolen cat for our first assignment! But wait. This one's bound to be better."

Jessica opened the notecard and read, " 'My parents just split up. Please write a brief letter to my father wishing him a happy birthday. I'm so mad at him right now that I can't stand writing to him myself.' "

"That sounds easy enough," Elizabeth commented.

"But doesn't it just make you itch to know why he can't stand to write even a birthday card?" Jessica asked, her eyes twinkling merrily. "This almost makes me feel like a detective. These letters are like clues to people's personal lives. People we'll probably never meet."

"Put away your spyglass and read the next request," Elizabeth teased. "We promised turnaround in one week, but I'm never going to have time to write the letters if you speculate on every single one."

Jessica rolled her eyes. "I can't help it. Inquiring minds want to know. . . ."

"Let me read this one," Elizabeth said, picking up the third letter. "Listen to this. 'My girlfriend is upset because I forgot that yesterday was the first anniversary of the day we met in science class last year. Will you please write her a romantic letter apologizing for me? Then I'll send it to her with a bouquet of flowers.' "

"Nice guy," Jessica snorted. "Hope he remembers the flowers."

Elizabeth punched her playfully on the arm. "You're terrible!"

"I know. Here's the last one," Jessica said as she opened it. "Uh-oh."

"What?"

"This woman says, 'I'm leaving my husband for another man. I'm getting the next train out of Sweet Valley and I won't be back. I'm enclosing his address and an extra five dollars. Please write to him and tell him not to come looking for me.' "

"Wow!" Elizabeth exclaimed. "I hope we don't get too many like this one."

"Oh, I don't know," Jessica said, fanning out the five five-dollar bills in her hand. "We said on the flyers that no problem was too large, no letter impossible to write."

Elizabeth grinned and snapped the money with her finger. "No financial goal too far out of reach," she added. "Let's get writing!" She walked over and sat down at the computer, fingers poised above the keys.

"How does this sound?" Jessica said, lifting the last request and pacing back and forth dramatically. " 'You must be a real jerk if your wife left you and doesn't even have the nerve to tell you herself!' "

"A little harsh, Jess," Elizabeth admonished. "You have to be tactful. How's this? 'Dear John, Don't call me, I'll call you. On second thought— no, I won't!' "

" 'And by the way, John,' " Jessica added,

shaking her finger at the letter in her hand, " 'have you seen any stray cats lately?' "

The twins burst out laughing.

"But seriously, Jess," Elizabeth said, "these people are counting on us. Let's write the easy ones first, the ones to the father and the girlfriend. Then we'll tackle the catnapper and the soon-to-be-lonely husband."

For the next hour, Jessica and Elizabeth wrote responses to the requests. When they were finished and satisfied, Jessica addressed the envelopes back to the senders with the exception of the one to the husband. That one she addressed directly to him.

"I'll give them to Mr. Ramsey, the mailman, on the way to school tomorrow. With luck, these people should have their responses by the day after tomorrow, well before when we promised them. Then I'll pick up the new requests after school."

"Don't get your hopes up, Jess," Elizabeth cautioned. "These four requests could have been a fluke—the beginning and end of our business."

"Oh, I don't know," Jessica said. "Remember Shelley saying the other day that Annie and Tony were having trouble? And Jennifer Mitchell was complaining about John Pfeifer the other day in gym. She said he was getting way too bossy with her. Who knows? We might become experts at writing Dear John letters."

"Maybe," Elizabeth said. "Wait a minute. John and Jennifer? It can't be. I see them all the time. They act like they're very together—always holding hands and gazing into each other's eyes, that sort of thing. Looks like paradise to me."

"You never know when there'll be trouble in paradise," Jessica reminded her.

Elizabeth grinned and shook her head. "And I suppose *we'll* be there to write the rejection letters when the time comes?"

"You have to have faith!" Jessica twirled and spread her arms wide. "I can feel it already. It's easy, fun, and *very* profitable. This is going to be the best business ever!"

Elizabeth wasn't thinking about the letter-writing service on Wednesday when Shelley walked into the photography lab. Elizabeth was up to her elbows in proofs for the swim team layout in the yearbook.

"Hi, Shelley, how's it going?" she greeted her friend.

"Good," Shelley said. "Where's the rest of the photography club? Didn't you have a meeting?"

"We sure did, but everyone went their separate ways and left me with this pile of swim shots."

"Everyone?" Shelley asked, looking around. "Isn't Jim here? He asked me to meet him after I got done with basketball practice."

"Oops," Elizabeth said, digging in her backpack. "I almost forgot." She pulled out a folded piece of paper. "Jim asked me to give this to you."

Shelley unfolded the paper and read Jim's message. Then she crumpled it and tossed it halfway across the room into the garbage can.

"Nice shot," Elizabeth said.

"I wish it were Jim's head," Shelley said. "But no, if it were Jim's head, I'd dribble it around first."

"Sounds pretty serious," Elizabeth commented. "Are you and Jim having trouble?"

"I honestly don't know, Liz," Shelley told her, her expression glum. "His note said he had to do some extra shots to go with a story he's working on for *The Oracle*." Shelley paused and sighed. "I just don't know what to think anymore. I'm beginning to wonder if Jim's avoiding me on purpose."

"I'm sorry I was the bearer of bad news," Elizabeth said, laying her hand on Shelley's arm. "But Jim really did have to retake some pictures for the paper. The chemicals were too strong when he tried to develop the first roll and some of his negatives got fried. I think he's just too preoccupied with work right now."

Shelley sat down on the stool next to Elizabeth, her shoulders slumped. "Todd told me the same thing—that Jim was probably just so obsessed about this yearbook project and the paper that he didn't notice anything else going on around him."

"Todd's a pretty smart guy—and he's had experience in being single-minded about things!"

Shelley smiled. "He mentioned something about the time he and Bruce tried to outdo each other."

Elizabeth rolled her eyes and nodded. "Good example. What is it about Bruce that brings out the worst in people? First Todd with that crazy fraternity rush, and then Jessica with that Club X disaster."

"Oh, Liz, I wish my relationship with Jim was as good as yours is with Todd," Shelley blurted out suddenly. "I really envy you."

"Todd and I have had our ups and downs," Elizabeth hastened to reassure her. "We've broken up more than once. We're *not* perfect."

"But Todd would never have run out on you if he knew you were coming to pick him up," Shelley countered. She began to walk around the photography room, picking up a photograph here and there but not really looking at them. "He would have waited and explained in person why he had to go," Shelley went on.

"Well, maybe," Elizabeth said. "Todd may have waited, or maybe even asked if I wanted to go along with him, but that doesn't mean Jim doesn't care. He's just compulsive about his photography, that's all."

Shelley stopped pacing and put her hands flat on the table as she faced Elizabeth. "Do you know how lucky you are?" she asked. "Todd is handsome and kind, smart and athletic. And it's obvious that he adores you."

Elizabeth walked around the table and placed a comforting hand on Shelley's shoulder. "I know how lucky I am, but even Todd has his moments of insensitivity. In fact, there have been times when he's been downright rude and I wondered what I ever saw in him!"

"I can't believe that," Shelley said flatly. "I just

wish Jim would take a few lessons from Todd. He could learn a lot."

"No one is perfect, Shel," Elizabeth continued. "My advice, if you want it, is that you wait until this whole yearbook mess is over, and then find some quiet, private time to talk over your feelings with Jim. I'm sure things will work out between you."

Shelley sighed. "I hope you're right."

Four

Before either Jessica or Elizabeth realized it, the first week of their business had flown by.

"Ten more requests," Jessica said aloud to herself as she dropped her books on her bed Friday afternoon. "Thirty-two in all since Tuesday."

As far as Jessica was concerned, this was the best, most lucrative idea that she had ever come up with. Of course, there had been some difficult letters. Like the one they had received from a man who had quit his job and then wanted the service to let his boss know exactly why.

"He wants us to be rude," Elizabeth had gasped when she read the letter. "Look at the language he uses."

"*We* don't have to use profanity to get his point across," Jessica had told her. "In fact, he'll probably be grateful if we can explain why he quit but still keep him on good enough terms with his boss so that he doesn't lose a reference."

Elizabeth had shaken her head in dismay. "Somehow I don't think he cares about getting a good reference. He just wants to lash out."

Both girls had sat in silence then, each trying to come up with a way to fulfill the man's request. "I have a good idea," Jessica had finally said. "Let's write two letters. One can be obnoxious and rude, without bad language, of course, and the other can be strongly worded but tactful. We'll send them both to him and let *him* choose."

"But we'll never know which letter he chose," Elizabeth had remarked. "What if he sends the rude one?"

"He's an adult. That's his choice. But I have a feeling that he'll see past his anger and choose the tactful letter."

They had agreed and written both letters, satisfied that they had done their best.

All we have to do is keep doing our best, Jessica thought as she spread Friday's mail on her rumpled brown bedspread. *I definitely should redecorate*, she added to herself. She looked at her chaotic surroundings with a critical eye. Her brown walls and accessories, which used to charge her full of rebellious pride, now looked dull and lifeless. "Red!" she said, nodding her head as she imagined bright cherry-colored walls, rugs, and a bedspread. Maybe she would make enough money from her share of Letters R Us to redo her room, too! She might even ask her mother for help.

Jessica forced herself to concentrate once again on the letters. She wanted to have them all sorted by the time Elizabeth got home from watching Todd's basketball practice.

I just hope we don't get any more letters like the one from the disgruntled employee, Jessica thought. Then she sighed. "Give me a batch of stolen cats and mother-in-law birthdays anytime," she said out loud.

She picked up the first letter. It was a request from an executive for a thank-you letter to the clerks in her office. The second was from a teen-ager wanting to ask a girl to go out with him.

"Silly boy," Jessica told the letter. "Just call her up!"

Then she picked up the third letter. She glanced at the return address. Shelley Novak! This was the first letter they had received from someone at Sweet Valley High, and Jessica ripped it open eagerly.

Dear Letters R Us, I'm a junior at Sweet Valley High, Shelley had written. *And lately I've developed an enormous crush on the boyfriend of one of my friends. I don't know how it happened. It's like, one day I woke up and realized how much I like him. He's really gorgeous—*

Who could this guy be? Jessica wondered. Cathy Ulrich was Shelley's best friend. Could Shelley have fallen for Cathy's boyfriend, Tim, who was a freshman at UCLA? Shelley's next words not only answered Jessica's question, but took her breath away.

He's tall, with brown hair and eyes, and he's the star forward of the boys' basketball team. He's incredibly nice, too. Whenever we talk, I know that he's really listening. He makes me feel so alive!

"Oh no!" Jessica gasped, tossing the letter on the bed as if it would burn her. "She's talking about Todd!" But then she gave in to her curiosity and picked up the letter again.

I can't bring myself to say anything to him about my feelings, so I thought it might be better to send him a letter. I feel so terrible about this crush, and I don't want to hurt my friend, but I can't deny my feelings, can I?

"Why not?" Jessica muttered. "Elizabeth doesn't deserve this."

He's the most wonderful boy on earth, and I'd like to let him know how I feel and find out whether he feels anything for me, Shelley continued. *Enclosed is five dollars. Can you help me?*

No! No! No! Jessica's mind screamed. What was she going to do? Shelley Novak had fallen head over heels in love with Todd Wilkins! Elizabeth would simply die!

Jessica's quick mind created and dismissed a million possibilities in a split second. She should tell Elizabeth. No, she couldn't tell Elizabeth. She could write a letter back to Shelley herself. No, she wouldn't write the letter. Maybe if she did nothing, Shelley would think her request had gotten lost in the mail. But then Shelley might write to Todd herself. Maybe she could send the money back and tell Shelley to forget the whole thing, that Todd wasn't for her. But then Shelley would know who was behind the letter-writing service.

It was an impossible situation. But if anyone was experienced at getting out of impossible situations, it was Jessica Wakefield. She had the brains and she had the nerve. Hadn't she proven Bruce Patman wrong when he had said that girls weren't brave enough to join Club X? Hadn't she told off super soap hunk Brandon Hunter on national television after she'd found out that he was just dating her as a publicity stunt? She simply needed time to think.

Elizabeth, however, didn't give her that time. A second later Jessica heard her sister knock on her door. "Jessica, are you in there? Did you bring home the requests?"

"Come on in," Jessica said, quickly stuffing Shelley's letter under a pile of clothes on the floor.

"I don't know how you find anything in here," Elizabeth commented as she came in.

Jessica grinned. "It's only a matter of memorizing my messes. If you want a certain book, just ask me. If you're looking for a purse or a particular pair of shoes, I can point you right to them. By the way, what do you think of red? I'm considering a total redo."

"Before you start stripping paint," Elizabeth said with a laugh, "could you point out the pile of requests that we got today? Did you say there were ten?"

"Uh . . ." Jessica thought quickly. Why had she stopped back at school to tell her sister how many letters there were? She knew why. She had been so excited about how successful their venture was becoming that she hadn't been able to wait to tell Elizabeth the news. "Uh . . . ten, yes. But, um, I had to go back to my locker to pick up something and I must have left one there. I've only got nine with me."

Elizabeth spotted the stack of letters on Jessica's wrinkled bedspread and picked them up. "Well, be sure to bring it home tomorrow. After all, we promised a response within the week."

"Tomorrow's Saturday," Jessica reminded her.

"I know. But didn't you tell me that the cheerleaders have a makeup practice scheduled for Saturday?"

"Oh, right," Jessica conceded. "I forgot. I guess I'll bring the letter home tomorrow, then."

Before tomorrow, I'll come up with a plan! Jessica thought as Elizabeth left the room. She dug Shelley's letter out from under the pile of clothes and thought about whom she might ask for advice. Lila? Amy? Her mother? Steven?

That was it—she'd call Steven. He was levelheaded about things like this. He was mature—a college man. She shuffled aside a bunch of papers and moved a stack of CDs to find her phone, then dialed the number of Steven's dorm.

"Is Steven Wakefield there?" she asked when a boy answered. She could hear the din of activity in the background.

"I'll get him," he told her. "Hey, Wakefield!" he bellowed down the hall. "Phone for you!"

Luckily, Jessica knew by now to hold the phone

away from her ear the second the person on the other end said "I'll get him." She had been blasted only once, and that was all it took. While she waited, she imagined having a red phone—then decided that maybe a purple and silver color scheme might look even better.

"This is Steven," her brother said a few moments later.

"Hi, big brother. Got a minute?"

"Ten, if you need them," Steven said. "What's up, Jess?"

"Our letter-writing service is going really well," Jessica began. "So well, in fact, that we've already made over a hundred and fifty dollars."

"Wow! Need another partner?"

"No, thanks. That's not the problem. We're keeping up with the volume. It's just that I got this letter from one of Liz's friends at school, and the girl has fallen in love with Todd."

"Oh," Steven said slowly. "That *is* a problem. What did Elizabeth say?"

"I haven't told her yet. I *was* just going to make the letter disappear, you know, thinking maybe the girl would get over her crush."

"But . . . ?"

"But I made the mistake of telling Elizabeth how many letters we received today, and she asked about the missing letter."

"So what are you going to do?" Steven asked.

"I thought you might have an idea," Jessica said hopefully.

"I'd probably tell her the whole story and let her decide," Steven said without hesitation.

"What if it ruins her friendship with Shelley? I mean, Shelley will probably get over this crush the minute she realizes that Todd is madly in love with Elizabeth, but if I tell Liz, then they'll probably have it out, and *poof!* The end of a friendship. And to make everything worse, Shelley already *has* a boyfriend."

"Hmm. That *does* complicate matters. Are you afraid that Elizabeth might go to this boyfriend and tell him about Shelley's letter?" Steven asked.

"Who knows what a woman trying to protect her relationship will do?" Jessica said dramatically. "If some girl was trying to put the moves on Sam, I'd do anything I had to do to keep him."

"So if you don't want to come clean to Elizabeth, and you don't want to show her the letter, what's the solution?"

Jessica twirled the phone cord around her finger, twisting it until it made a huge, wrapped package around her whole hand. "I've got it!" she cried out. "I'll rewrite Shelley's letter! Liz will never know it was from a friend. And I'll change enough of the details so that she doesn't know the letter is referring to Todd, either. You know, the names will be changed to protect the guilty."

"Well, it sounds a little complicated," Steven said. "But it'll probably work. Liz will write the letter to a bogus person. Don't forget to change the address on the envelope, too."

"I won't. And then before I mail it, I'll switch the letter into another envelope and mail it to Shelley. And if Shelley *does* decide to mail it to Todd—which I'm sure she won't—he'll probably just be flattered, and that will be the end of the whole thing."

"Right," Steven said firmly.

"After all, Elizabeth and Todd's relationship is so strong," Jessica added, "what possible harm can one little letter do?"

Five

"Elizabeth," Jessica wailed. "This girl barely knows the guy. Don't make the letter so romantic!"

"Why not?" Elizabeth asked, chuckling at Jessica's reluctance. "This girl is in *love*. Maybe she *thinks* all she wants to do is send the boy a letter to tell him about her feelings, but what she really wants is for him to fall for her, too. Am I right?"

"Possibly," Jessica said, her expression doubtful. *If you only knew*, she thought. "On the other hand, maybe she's hoping we won't even write the letter. You know, so that she won't wind up being embarrassed. You know as well as I do, Elizabeth, that sometimes just seeing something on paper is enough to make you realize how wrong you've been about it."

Elizabeth shook her head. "I don't know what you're talking about, Jess. I've never seen you act so strange about a request before. You didn't think twice about socking it to that guy's horrible boss the other day."

"That was different. I . . . uh . . . I just want our customers to be satisfied, that's all," Jessica explained lamely. *What am I supposed to tell her?* Jessica thought. *That if she doesn't tone it down, she'll be helping Shelley Novak take her own boyfriend away?*

"How does this sound?" Elizabeth asked. " 'I know you think of me as only a friend, but friendships can grow into much more. We have so many things in common—our love of sports, our appreciation for beautiful sunsets on the beach, moonlight strolls along the water—that maybe it's time we thought about taking the next step.' "

"You can't say that!" Jessica cried. "How do you *know* he likes moonlight strolls and sunsets?"

"Who doesn't? Todd sure does," Elizabeth argued.

"That's beside the point," Jessica said, stomping over to the bed and sitting down. Elizabeth was impossible! She was projecting all of Todd's likes into the letter. Why didn't she just hand Todd over to Shelley on a silver platter?

"What *is* the point?" Elizabeth asked.

"You don't know that *this* guy likes them, and the girl didn't say anything about beaches. Why don't you just say . . ." She put her fingers to her temples and massaged them as she thought. "Say, 'I'll bet we have a lot in common. Maybe we should get together sometime. I'll see you around.' "

Elizabeth laughed. "That's *boring*. He won't be interested in her at all if I just write that."

"But what about his girlfriend?" Jessica stood and looked out Elizabeth's window, trying desperately to think of something that would persuade Elizabeth to make the letter less romantic. "Haven't you thought about her? How would you, I mean *she*, feel if she knew you were writing the most romantic letter possible to try to help someone else take your—I mean, her boyfriend away?"

"If their love is strong, then there won't be a problem," Elizabeth said with certainty. "But maybe the boyfriend is sending out signals to this other girl that he's ready for a change."

Jessica groaned and rolled her eyes.

"Are you OK, Jess?"

I would be more OK if you would stop writing that letter! "Fine," Jessica answered. "Just tone it down a little more, please." *Tone it down a lot more!* she silently begged.

"So I should take out this part about how she's been watching him from afar, hoping against hope that he'll notice her?"

"You should *definitely* take *that* out," Jessica said, sighing. "Even *I* would be embarrassed to tell a guy that."

"Oh, Jess," Elizabeth said as she deleted the paragraph, "I can't imagine you ever being embarrassed about anything, especially if it had to do with a guy."

47

Jessica had to laugh. "Well, that's true," she admitted.

Jessica threw herself down on Elizabeth's neatly spread comforter. She might as well give up. Besides, what did it matter? The gushier it was, the more likely it was that Todd would think it was a joke and simply throw it away.

"How's Sam, by the way?" Elizabeth asked.

"I haven't seen much of Sam lately. Not since the concert. This letter-writing service is keeping us pretty busy, in case you haven't noticed."

"I haven't seen much of Todd lately, either," Elizabeth said. "Between school, homework, the newspaper, and the yearbook, I'm swamped. I *know* he'll appreciate all the time I had to spend away from him, though, when he sees the warmup jacket I've ordered."

Jessica rolled over to look directly at her sister.

"Just remember the reason you're giving him the jacket," she said. "Because you felt bad for spending so much time away from him while you were working on the harassment article."

"I know. But it won't be for very much longer," Elizabeth said optimistically as she turned back to her desk. "Besides, Todd's very understanding."

"I hope so," Jessica mumbled.

"Did you say something?" Elizabeth asked, swiveling around again in her chair, her head framed by the screen on which was written the love letter she was about to send to her very understanding boyfriend.

"Not a thing," Jessica said, hoping that the wall

behind her sister would come to life and swallow Elizabeth's computer. "I'm just talking to myself."

Though on the surface nothing had changed, Shelley felt different. No one sitting in the Sweet Valley High cafeteria on Monday knew what Shelley had done—not even her best friend, Cathy—but that didn't stop her from feeling self-conscious. She hadn't yet received a letter back from the letter-writing service, the one that would tell Todd of her feelings, but already she was questioning her judgment.

Shelley sipped her milk and wondered what the letter would say. Then, almost immediately, she wondered what Todd would think of her when he read it. Fantasies wove their way into her mind, hinting at the possibilities to come.

Todd would never make her feel stupid for sending the letter, she decided. He would appreciate her honesty. Probably nothing would come of it, but who knew? She hadn't seen Todd and Elizabeth together much lately. Maybe everything wasn't perfect for them, either. Maybe the time was right for a change.

Shelley shook her head, clearing her thoughts. Change was good, wasn't it? No one wanted to stagnate. You had to keep moving, keep experimenting, keep experiencing. That's what life was all about—moving on.

But did she really *want* to move on? More to the point, did she want to leave Jim behind? Even though he hadn't been spending a lot of time with her lately, there had been something so special and beautiful about her relationship with Jim. She didn't want to lose the chance of that returning, but she didn't want to hang onto a hollow shell of what once had been, either. Oh, she felt so guilty! She would keep this all a secret, just in case things didn't work out. Or *should* she ask Cathy for advice?

Shelley put her head in her hands and closed her eyes. She didn't have to make any major decisions over her lunch. She would wait until the letter came back from the service and then decide whether to send it or not.

"Hi, Shelley!" Elizabeth's voice broke through her concentration. "Aren't Mondays wild? Hey, congratulations on your win Friday night. I heard it was down to the absolutely last second."

Shelley jerked upright and glanced around to make sure this wasn't still part of her dream. "Uh, thanks," she said, motioning for Elizabeth to sit down. What else could she do? Elizabeth would think it was odd if she didn't invite her to join her.

"It's all over school about the way you scored the last basket as the clock ran out. John Pfeifer thought we should do a piece on it for the paper and he asked me to get the inside scoop. Did Jim get any photos?"

"Jim wasn't there," Shelley said, dipping her head to concentrate on her pasta.

"I'm sorry. Well, I'm glad Todd stayed to cheer you on," Elizabeth remarked.

"Me, too," Shelley said, choking on a noodle. Did it show? she worried. If she looked Elizabeth straight in the eye, would Elizabeth be able to tell that she was crazy about Todd? She had to change the subject.

But Elizabeth, unknowingly, was prolonging her discomfort.

"Speaking of Todd," Elizabeth said, looking around the cafeteria, "I wonder where he is? He was supposed to meet me here. When he comes, the two of you can give me a play-by-play account of the game for John. John would have talked to you himself, but he and Jennifer looked like they were having a pretty heavy-duty conversation. Anyway," Elizabeth went on blithely, "Todd should be here any second."

Great, Shelley thought. *Just what I need—to sit with Todd and Elizabeth.* What would Elizabeth think if she knew that Shelley was harboring a secret crush on her boyfriend? Worse yet, what would Elizabeth say if she knew that Shelley had actually done something about it, or at least was about to do something about it?

"It's too bad that the boys' team didn't make it to the playoffs or win the regional championship, like the girls' team did," Elizabeth went on relentlessly. "Then the school would have twice as much to celebrate. Todd says the boys' team needs to tighten up its defense and—"

"I think Jeffrey French might have gotten some pictures," Shelley blurted. What was sending the letter going to do to her friendship with Elizabeth? What would Jim say if he found out? Did she

51

really want it to be over between them? On the other hand, how could she continue the way things were—her relationship with Jim wilting, and her attraction to Todd growing—without doing something about it?

When Jessica entered the cafeteria, the first people she saw were Elizabeth and Shelley, their heads bent together, deep in conversation.

"Oh no!" she whispered to herself. "I never should have let Elizabeth mail those letters this morning. She probably recognized the address."

"What?" Lila asked, coming up behind her.

"Oh, nothing," Jessica muttered. She tried to appear calm as she waited in the food line, but her thoughts were in turmoil. The night before, she had managed to switch the envelope that Elizabeth had made out to the phony address with the envelope addressed to Shelley, and she'd hidden it in the middle of the stack of responses. She'd had to stay up until midnight to do it and sneak into Elizabeth's room while she slept, but she had congratulated herself on a job well done. The final step of the plan had been to grab the letters and deliver them to the post office herself before school in the morning.

Then Elizabeth had blown her plan away. "I'm driving right by the post office," she had informed a sleepy Jessica the next morning. "I'll drop off the letters for you."

"No, that's OK," Jessica had told her, hurriedly getting out of bed. "It's my part of the partnership."

Elizabeth had smiled that maddeningly sincere smile she always bestowed on someone when she was gladly doing them a favor. "It's no problem, and besides, isn't Lila picking you up today? She might get suspicious if you ask her to stop by the post office."

Nothing Jessica had said could persuade Elizabeth to change her mind, and Jessica had worried all morning that her kind-hearted twin would find the envelope addressed to Shelley and figure the whole mess out.

Now, glancing at Elizabeth and Shelley across the crowded lunchroom, she was sure that was exactly what had happened. Elizabeth was waving her arms frantically in the air and Shelley was standing up and leaning across the table, her face right in Elizabeth's face. It didn't look good.

"Listen, Lila," she said as she paid for her lunch, "go ahead and find a table. I have to go talk to Liz for a minute."

She didn't even wait to hear Lila's reply. The only thing she could think about was getting to Elizabeth's table to defuse the coming explosion.

A few seconds later she skidded to a halt next to Elizabeth. Her sister and Shelley stared up at her with questioning eyes.

"Is anything the matter, Jess?" Elizabeth asked, her voice calm.

Jessica looked back and forth between the two girls.

"Yeah, you look upset," Shelley added. "Want to join us?"

"Well . . . uh . . . I thought you two were . . ."

53

Jessica stammered. "What were you talking about just now?" she finally managed to ask.

"The game last Friday," Elizabeth told her, clearly still puzzled by her twin's sudden appearance. "Shelley was giving me the highlights. John Pfeifer wanted this story from the personal angle. He sent me to get the player's scoop on the game."

Jessica remembered Elizabeth's waving arms and Shelley's jumping up and down and immediately felt foolish. Elizabeth *couldn't* know of Shelley's letter or she wouldn't be sitting with her and discussing the game. The secret was safe, at least for now. "Oh," was all Jessica managed to say.

"Are you sure you're feeling all right?" Shelley asked Jessica.

"I'm fine, really," Jessica said. "Well, listen," she added as she backed away, "I'll be going." She took another step. "Lila has a table saved. I'll see you later."

"Bye," Elizabeth and Shelley said in unison. Jessica felt Elizabeth's eyes on her back as she affected a nonchalant stroll over to where Lila and Amy were sitting with some of their crowd. So much for her attempt to save the day. She had only made a fool of herself.

Six

"Money, money, money, but not an ounce of time," Jessica moaned on Tuesday.

"I thought that you *wanted* to make money," Elizabeth teased, waving the latest pile of five-dollar bills in Jessica's face. "I know I sure did."

"I *do* want to make money, but not at the expense of my social life. I haven't seen Sam in over a week!"

"Yeah, but remember, Sam's been busy, too. He was preparing for a race all last week, and on Sunday he drove all the way to San Diego for the big day. You wouldn't have seen him even if we hadn't been working."

Jessica frowned. "I guess you're right," she said. "But what about you and Todd?"

"Now, *that's* a different story," Elizabeth admitted. "Todd's wanted to get together more than a few times in the last week, but I had to put him off each time because of the letters. In fact, I'm going to have to call him up tonight to break a date just so I can catch up. Who would have thought that so many people hated to write?"

Elizabeth swiveled back around in her desk chair and flipped on her computer. Jessica came up behind her and put her hand on her shoulder. "Why don't you leave the letters for tonight and go out with Todd? We can catch up tomorrow."

"No, by then we'll be even further behind." Elizabeth sighed. "Todd will understand."

Just then, Elizabeth's phone rang. She picked it up. "Oh, hi, Todd," she said.

"All ready to go to Howard's?" Todd asked.

"We're going to the *deli?*"

"I thought we'd stop there and pick up some of our favorite cheesecake before we head out to the beach," Todd explained.

Todd's deep voice gave Elizabeth a warm feeling, and she almost gave in to the temptation to go out that evening. Then she glanced at the growing pile of letters on her desk.

Elizabeth cleared her throat. "Todd, I'm sorry, but I can't make it this evening. I have a *pile* of stuff to do."

"Is this a pile that I can help you with on the way to the deli?" Todd teased. "Even famous writers have to eat, you know."

"Famous writer," Elizabeth scoffed. "I wish!"

"You are, you know. How many other high school juniors can say they've had feature articles in the *Los Angeles Times?*"

Elizabeth laughed. "Not many, I guess. But I still can't go out tonight. I'm swamped."

"You've been swamped for the past week," Todd said. "What's keeping you so busy?"

"Writing," Elizabeth replied quickly. At least that much was true. She didn't want to tell him what she was actually doing because she wanted the business to be an absolute secret. It wasn't that she thought Todd would blow their cover; it was that she wanted the money she earned and the present she bought him with it to be a complete surprise.

"Writing what?" Todd asked. "An article for a national magazine?"

"Hardly," Elizabeth joked. "It's much closer to home. I *am* getting paid for it, though."

"You have me curious now, Liz. This must be some really big secret if you can't even tell your boyfriend."

"Sort of." She smiled into the phone. "I'll give you a hint. What I'm doing will benefit you in the very near future."

"Benefit me? How?" Todd asked, obviously intrigued.

"All I can tell you is that there are great things to come."

"You sound like a fortune cookie, Liz!" Todd sighed dramatically. "Since you won't go out with me and you won't tell me why except to allude to surprises in my future, I guess I'll have to concede defeat."

"You're hardly defeated," Elizabeth admonished playfully. As she was talking she booted up the word-processing program on her computer. She opened a file to begin the first letter.

"Not defeated, maybe. Just alone and hungry. Promise me that, no matter what, you'll save Saturday afternoon for me. I have something very special planned."

"I'm sure I'll be caught up by then," Elizabeth said somewhat absently, her mind already spinning with ways to answer the first new request.

"I hope so," Todd said softly in that special husky voice of his that usually made her feel all snuggly inside. "I miss you, Liz."

"Me, too," she replied, this time hardly even noticing his tone. "See you tomorrow."

But the next day Elizabeth was equally swamped, and for the rest of the week she and Jessica worked crazily, answering letters and shuttling back and forth to the post office. By the time Saturday arrived, Elizabeth was really looking forward to some time off with Todd.

"I feel as if we should get one of those magnetic signs that says 'Mail Service—Makes Frequent Stops' and put it on the side of our Jeep," Jessica complained good-naturedly as she walked into Elizabeth's room late Saturday morning. "The only difference between our vehicle and the ones the mail carriers use is that our steering wheel isn't on the right-hand side."

"I'll bet you never thought Letters R Us would become this successful," Elizabeth commented as she lay back on her bed and crossed her feet at the ankles.

"Never in a million years," Jessica agreed. "I love how much money we're making, but I'm getting kind of burned out."

"Me, too," Elizabeth said. "I'm ready for a break. I wonder what Todd has planned for this afternoon?"

Jessica went back out into the hallway and brought in a canvas mailbag tied with a drawstring at the top. "I know what *we* have planned for this morning," she said, loosening the tie and dumping the contents onto Elizabeth's stomach.

Elizabeth sat up and stared at the huge pile of letters now scattered all over her bed. She groaned. "Todd is going to throw a fit when I cancel out on him again. I'm beginning to wonder whether we should consider hiring some help. How about Enid? Or Penny? Or Olivia? They're all good writers."

"And split the profits?" Jessica cried. "How dare you even suggest such a thing! Here, I'll help. We can whip these out in no time at all and you'll still be able to keep your date with Todd."

"I don't know if you've noticed, Jess, but it takes more time than you think to write these letters. I've been staying up late every night. Whenever I'm not doing homework, I'm pounding out letters on the computer."

Jessica's mouth turned down. "Are you implying that I'm not carrying my half of the workload?" she asked.

"No, that's not it at all," Elizabeth assured her. "I know you're putting in just as much time as I am, running back and forth to the post office and sorting through the letters, not to mention helping me decide what to write and keeping track of the bookkeeping. I'm just saying that we don't have *lives* anymore."

Jessica counted the requests blanketing Elizabeth's bed. "With what I counted last night and today's haul, we need only another hundred dollars to meet our financial goal. After that, we can slow down or hire some help. Fair enough?"

"Fair enough," Elizabeth agreed. "Let's get a move on. Maybe you're right and we can get these finished before my three o'clock date with Todd."

"OK," Jessica said, tearing open an envelope. She scanned the page and then read the letter aloud.

When she had finished, Elizabeth sighed. "That's a pretty bizarre request. Mr. Rosenthal wants us to write a letter of recommendation for his student intern mechanic at Rosenthal Motors. But from the letter, I get the impression that Mr. Rosenthal doesn't like him very much."

"I know," Jessica remarked, scanning the missive again. "But it *does* sound as if Mr. Rosenthal respects the student's work. I think we should stick to the facts and keep the emotion out of it. I mean, we don't have to have Mr. Rosenthal say that he's sorry to lose the guy or anything, just that his work was efficient and effective while he was training."

"Efficient and effective," Elizabeth repeated. "I like that!" She began tapping out the first paragraph of the letter.

" 'Dear Sir or Madam,' " Elizabeth murmured as she typed. " 'Jeffrey Burgett was an efficient and effective mechanic during his student internship at Rosenthal Motors. His work was exemplary . . ."

By the time Elizabeth and Jessica had finished about half of the letters, it was two o'clock.

"Oh, no!" Elizabeth exclaimed as she looked at the clock for the first time in several hours. "I can't believe how much time those letters took."

"Or how many more letters we have to write," Jessica said, flopping back on the floor and tossing the pile of letters skyward.

"I have to call Todd," Elizabeth said, reaching for the phone. "I hate to cancel out on him again, especially when he was so insistent I save Saturday for him. But I just can't see any other way to finish this mess before Monday!"

Jessica sighed. "Why are you so concerned with finishing by Monday? I think you should keep your date with Todd. The letters will wait one more day."

"*These* letters might wait," Elizabeth said. "But what about the new ones we get on Monday? This is not just a fluke, Jess. On Monday we may get even *more* mail than we got today. And I don't want to get so far behind that we can't ever catch up."

"I guess you're right," Jessica agreed reluctantly. "Listen, I'll go get us something to eat while you call Todd. We'll need our energy for the marathon ahead."

One thing about Jessica, Elizabeth thought as she punched in Todd's number, *she has incredible staying power if money is involved!* She hadn't left Elizabeth's side during this whole business venture, and Elizabeth had been sincere when she told her earlier that she was really doing her share of the work.

While the phone rang, Elizabeth nervously twirled the cord in her fingers. "Todd," she said when he answered.

"Hi, Liz," he replied. "I'm really looking forward to our date this afternoon."

Elizabeth had a sinking feeling in the bottom of her stomach. She loved Todd so much and she hated to disappoint him, even if it was for a good cause—the cause being him. "That's what I called to talk to you about," she began tentatively.

"We're going to have a great time," Todd broke in before she had a chance to tell him the bad news. "I rented your favorite romantic comedy, *Romancing the Stone.* I had to go all over town to find it at a video store, but I finally found a copy at Video Stop. And I bought your favorite cheesecake from Howard's Deli—just because you missed it the other night—*plus* a couple of bottles of sparkling apple cider. We can kick back, relax, and sip cider while we watch the villain get devoured by the crocodile."

"Wow," Elizabeth said nervously. "It sounds like you planned a really special afternoon." She paused and hoped that Todd would understand what she was about to do. "And that makes it even more difficult for me to tell you why I called," she continued.

"This doesn't sound good," Todd said lightly.

Elizabeth hesitated only a second and then plunged ahead. "I'm really sorry, Todd. I'm not going to be able to make it."

"Again?" Todd asked incredulously. "Why not?"

"Uh . . . Jessica and I are working on a project together and we're swamped." As soon as the words were out of her mouth, she wished she could take them back.

"Swamped!" Todd's voice doubled in volume. "You've been swamped all week. All last week, too!"

"It really is for a good cause," Elizabeth told him hurriedly. "I'm doing it all for you. You'll see."

"Well, I don't see now!" Todd remarked loudly. "Every time I want to see you you're super busy and all I've heard are lame excuses designed to keep me dangling. What gives, Elizabeth?" he demanded.

Elizabeth was stunned. "I don't appreciate being yelled at," she told him, her voice rising also. "I *told* you that I'm working on something secret, and I expect you to trust me enough to wait until I'm free to tell you all about it."

"Well, just how long am I supposed to wait? You've been *swamped* for *two solid weeks*. We barely see each other anymore, Liz, and I want to know why, that's all." Todd paused, and Elizabeth thought she could hear him thinking of what to say next. "I'm your boyfriend," he finally continued. "We're supposed to be in love. I think I have a right to know."

"A *right* to know?" Elizabeth sputtered. *And to think I'm doing all this just to buy him a special present!* she thought angrily.

And then she went on. "*I* have a right to some secrets in my private life, Todd. And I have a right to have some secrets even from you! If you can't understand that, then we don't have anything further to say to each other!"

"If that's the way you want it, Liz," Todd said, his voice strangely calm. "When—if—you have a spare second, give me a call."

Elizabeth slammed the receiver down. "Todd Wilkins," she said aloud, "sometimes you can be the most exasperating boy on earth!"

Seven

Shelley stood outside Todd Wilkins's front door, her finger hovering over the doorbell. Should she ring it? Should she turn around before it was too late and run for home? What was she doing there, anyway?

Shelley had been asking herself the same questions for the past five minutes. It had been much easier to talk herself into going over to Todd's house with the excuse of returning the basketball bloopers video that he had loaned her when she was sitting in the safety and comfort of her own bedroom. Talking to her own reflection in the mirror had not been nearly as scary as staring at the Wilkinses' closed front door.

"Novak, this is ridiculous!" she muttered. "You're here. He hasn't received the letter yet, because you only sent it this morning. This is a perfectly innocent, friendly visit. He probably won't even ask you in. Now ring the bell before Mr. Wilkins notices you hanging around on their front porch and calls the police!"

Before she had the chance to talk herself out of it again, Shelley reached out and rang the bell. To her ears the chime was deafening.

Why aren't you with Jim? her inner voice taunted her as she heard footsteps coming to the front door. Her mouth went suddenly dry and she took a step back, intending to run. But she took one look at Todd's surprised face and her feet felt like lead.

"Shelley! Hi!" he greeted her with a smile. "What brings you here?"

For an entire three seconds, Shelley wasn't sure she could make her vocal cords function. Then she swallowed hard and smiled back. "I was in the neighborhood and thought I'd drop off your bloopers video." She held it out to him. "It was really funny. Thanks for lending it to me."

"You're welcome," Todd said. As he reached for the video his hand brushed hers, and Shelley felt the shock wave tingle all the way up her arm. She pulled her hand back quickly, hoping he hadn't noticed her reaction.

Shelley racked her brain for something intelligent to say. She had never really talked to Todd alone, away from school. Talking to him on the bleachers during practice or when she and Jim were together with Todd and Elizabeth was a totally different experience. It was *much, much* easier. "I really liked the part where Kareem Abdul-

Jabbar jumped for the basket and sailed right past it," she finally said.

"My favorite part is the slam-dunk footage. All those guys shattering the backboards—it's amazing how much power they have."

"Could you imagine the look on Coach Tilman's face if one of us shattered a backboard?" Shelley said. "He'd have the person's head on a platter."

"Diced," Todd added for good measure. "Hey, great game last night. Your offense is hard to beat. All the other teams in California should just quit right now and give Sweet Valley the trophy."

Shelley smiled at Todd's exaggerated praise.

"Thanks. That would save us *all* a lot of trouble, wouldn't it?"

"Life wouldn't be nearly as much fun, though, without the games," Todd said.

The subject of basketball exhausted, they stood there awkwardly until Shelley said, "Well, I guess I'd better be going." She began to back off the porch, hoping she was exiting with dignity.

"Hey, wait a second," Todd said. "Um . . . are you busy this afternoon? I was just about to watch a movie and have a snack, but it would be more fun with a friend."

"What about Elizabeth?" Shelley asked shyly, and then wished she hadn't asked at all.

Todd's expression was carefully blank. "Oh, she couldn't make it because of some project she's working on with Jessica." Todd shrugged. "I'd hate to see good cheesecake go to waste. C'mon."

He opened the door wide and motioned her to come inside.

Oh well, why not? Shelley thought. This was what she had been hoping for, wasn't it? A chance to spend more time with Todd. Shelley smiled and nodded. "Sure. We wouldn't want good food and a good movie to go to waste."

When she walked into Todd's living room she immediately felt self-conscious. It was obvious that Todd had gone to great lengths to create a romantic atmosphere. The curtains were drawn and the lights turned down low. On the coffee table was a tray of sliced meats and cheeses, a cheesecake, two plates, two stemmed goblets, and a bottle of sparkling apple cider chilling in an ice bucket.

Elizabeth is a fool, Shelley thought. Todd had planned and created the perfect date and Elizabeth had canceled out at the last minute because of a project with her sister. She was a fool *and* crazy.

"Have a seat," Todd invited, showing her to one end of the plush sofa. "Would you like some cider?"

"I'd love some," Shelley found herself saying. As she accepted the goblet of bubbly liquid, she contemplated the wisdom of sitting there in the semidarkness with the boy she had a crush on.

I really should be doing this with Jim, she told herself as she sipped the cider and let the bubbles tickle her nose. *And Todd should be here with Elizabeth.* She knew she had just happened along at the right moment and that she was Todd's second choice of companion, but as Todd sat down comfortably next to her and started the movie she threw all thoughts of right and wrong away.

Elizabeth had *chosen* not to keep her date with Todd. Jim had *chosen* to lock himself in his darkroom all weekend. It wasn't Shelley's or Todd's fault that they were thrown together, two lonely castoffs of love.

She knew she was being melodramatic, but it suited her mood. It also made it easier to sit next to Todd and imagine that he felt the same way about her as she felt about him.

"I like romantic comedies, don't you?" Todd remarked a few minutes into the movie.

"I do." Shelley blushed at the irony of her two words. "I mean, I always have," she hurried on. "And this one is one of my favorites. But I also like plain old slapstick."

"I'm a Laurel and Hardy fan myself," Todd commented.

Shelley smiled. "I like Abbott and Costello, too!" she said. "Jim kind of prefers documentaries," she added without thinking.

"That's the photographer in him," Todd said. "Elizabeth always dissects the screenplay. You know, she edits as she watches. I just like to watch." Todd grinned. "You can join me for a comedy anytime!"

Todd turned his attention back to the movie. Shelley glanced quickly at him, then away again before he could notice. Had he said what she thought he had said? Was he giving her an actual invitation to come watch a movie sometime? Or was he just being nice? It was hard to tell. Shelley wondered what would happen when Todd received her letter in a day or two.

A romantic scene came on the screen just then, and Shelley sat back. What would happen, she wondered, if she told Todd right then and there how she felt about him? Would he lean over to her like the hero in the movie and look longingly into her eyes? Would he put his arm around her and draw her close and tell her that she meant more to him than any treasure in the world, and what was happening between them was something so strong that neither one of them could fight it?

All of a sudden she felt her shoulder brush against Todd's. She turned to look at him, and at the same instant he turned to look at her. For a brief moment, their eyes locked.

A burst of mariachi music on the screen snapped her back to her senses. She pulled back as if scorched. Humiliated, she concentrated on the screen, hoping that in the dimness Todd couldn't see that her face matched the color of her hair. Had she leaned into him? Had he leaned into her? Was she as pathetically obvious to Todd as she appeared to herself? Good grief! What was she doing here?

"Great movie, huh?" Todd said, passing her a slice of cheesecake.

"The best," she said, feeling a little better. He didn't look at her strangely, or with pity. He was still Todd, her friend.

In companionable silence they watched the rest

of the movie. Afterward they shot a few baskets, and then Shelley headed for home.

"I had a great time today," she said as Todd walked her to her car. And then she found herself saying the strangest thing. "Say hi to Elizabeth for me. Tell her she missed a great movie."

"Yeah," Todd answered. "And thanks for the workout. I always enjoy getting creamed on my own basketball court."

"Happy to oblige you anytime," Shelley teased.

"Say hi to Jim," Todd called after her as she drove off.

"I will." *If I see him*, she thought. As she drove away Shelley found herself rehashing the afternoon. She couldn't believe how easy it had been to spend time alone with Todd. He had been as kind and friendly as she knew he would be. He had been fun to talk to. They liked so many of the same things—basketball, slapstick comedies, cheesecake. It *couldn't* have been just her imagination that he was attracted to her, too. Maybe, just maybe, she thought as she drove down to the beach and let the ocean breeze blow through her open windows, he was beginning to fall in love with her.

Well, you'll find out soon enough, Novak, Shelley told herself. *He should get your letter on Monday.*

Eight

Elizabeth was surprised when Todd joined her in the cafeteria for lunch on Monday. Hunched over an article she was editing for *The Oracle*, she didn't even notice him until he slid into the seat beside her and kissed her on the cheek.

"Oh, hi," she said, a bit nervously. She hadn't spoken to him since their phone fight on Saturday. She didn't know how *he* felt, but *she* felt ready to make up. She was just too busy lately to have to deal with another problem! "I'm sorry about canceling the other day," she plunged on, her smile tentative. "I hope you didn't let that cheesecake go to waste."

Todd opened up his sack lunch and laid it on the table. "Nope. All is forgiven. Shelley dropped by to return a video I'd lent her, and I made her stay and help me eat the feast."

"That's good," Elizabeth said, making a few

quick red marks on her paper. If she could just finish her preliminary corrections before lunch was over, she would be caught up—for the moment. "How's Shelley doing, anyway?" she asked, somewhat distractedly. "Have she and Jim worked things out?"

Tom shrugged. "I'm not sure. We didn't talk about Jim much. We were too busy watching the movie," he told her.

"Hmm," Elizabeth said, barely registering what Todd had said. She frowned at the article before her and made another series of corrections with her red pencil.

"You seem pretty busy today. *As usual*," Todd said suddenly.

"I am," Elizabeth replied, not looking up and choosing not to notice his change in tone. She did not want to get drawn into another senseless argument. "I feel as if I've been doing nothing but writing for weeks now. But as soon as I finish this article on athletes on drugs I'll have some free time. I hope."

"I thought you were going to ask Olivia to write that article," Todd said.

Elizabeth sighed. "I did, but she was totally wrapped up in putting out the next issue of *Visions*, and Penny wanted the article for this issue of *The Oracle*," she explained.

"And how long do you think *this* project will take?" Todd asked, his voice strained.

Elizabeth shrugged. "I don't know. I think I can get it done before the end of lunch if I keep working," she said.

73

Todd stood up. "I think I'll leave you, then," he said, gathering up his lunch with short, precise motions. "I wouldn't want to get in the way of your *work!*"

"OK," Elizabeth said. Then she stood up long enough to give him a brief kiss. She would *not* get into a fight! "I'll see you later," she said.

"I'll believe that when it happens," Todd grumbled as he strode off.

Elizabeth's lips tightened into a frown, and she forced herself to turn back to her article.

"Aha! I suspected as much." Jessica interrupted Elizabeth by tapping on her sister's work. "Todd walked out of the cafeteria in a major hurry, and so I figured you had your nose in a writing assignment. Haven't you heard? Boyfriends need to see your *face* once in a while to know you care. Otherwise they walk off in a huff."

Elizabeth looked up and glanced toward the cafeteria exit. "I can't imagine why he'd be mad," she protested. "He was probably just in a hurry to go somewhere."

"Ignore the signs if you want," Jessica said with a sigh. "From the expression *I* saw on his face, I think something is definitely wrong."

"Don't be silly, Jess. Todd's just been in a bit of a bad mood. And I really don't blame him for not wanting to hang around while I work. Everything is *fine*, Jess. Quit worrying."

But everything wasn't fine. When Jessica went to the post office on Wednesday to pick up their mail, she was shocked to find a letter in the stack with Todd's address on it. Hoping she was mistaken, she hurried out to the Jeep, sank down in the driver's seat, and ripped open the letter. She knew the minute she saw the handwriting that it was from Todd.

Dear Letters R Us, the letter began. *I've just received the most incredible love letter. The trouble is, the sender is a friend of my girlfriend. In fact, up until now, she and I have been good friends, too. We have a lot in common and get along well together. Even when she came over to my house the other day for a visit, she didn't let on that her feelings for me had grown to more than just friendship.*

Here's the problem. A couple of weeks ago I would have just brushed this off. I've been going steady with my girlfriend for a very long time and I thought we were very much in love. But lately, she's always tied up with something she's very secretive about—she tells me it's some sort of writing project—and I can't help but think she's interested in someone else. Maybe I'm crazy, but we're spending less and less time together, and it's becoming clear that the romance has gone out of our relationship.

Jessica took a deep breath and closed her eyes. This couldn't be happening. When she opened her eyes she would discover it had all been a big mistake. She opened her eyes, but Todd's words were still there on the paper, staring her in the face. And it only got worse as Jessica read on.

I think I should at least give this other girl a chance, if only to shake my girlfriend up. Who knows? I don't like to think it, but maybe our relationship really is finished after all this time.

"No, no, no, Todd," Jessica whispered. What she really wanted to do was *scream* at the letter. "You don't know what's going on. You're jumping to conclusions. Elizabeth still loves you! She's doing it all for you!"

Jessica reluctantly turned her attention back to the letter.

Will you please write two letters for me? Todd concluded. *One to my girlfriend, explaining that I think we should cool it for a while, and the other to my friend, to ask her out for next Friday.*

Jessica pinched the bridge of her nose hard to try to make her headache—the one that had come on the second that she tore open Todd's letter—go away. She had thought Shelley's letter was bad, but that had been simply a tremor compared with Todd's. Todd's was the earthquake. Todd's was off the Richter scale, and any minute now she was expecting California to slide right off into the Pacific Ocean, taking Jessica and her stupid idea about a letter-writing service with it.

"How could this have happened?" she asked herself about fifty times on the way home. "How could my plan have backfired so badly?" Todd was only supposed to be flattered by Shelley's letter and leave it at that. Instead, he was ready to break it off with Elizabeth. The awful, horrible, terrible, and ironic thing was that *Elizabeth* had written the very letter that had driven her own boyfriend away!

It was all too confusing, and Jessica knew that she had to do something to fix the dreadful situation without Elizabeth discovering the truth.

Jessica sped up, determined to get home as soon as she safely could. Elizabeth wasn't due home for at least another hour—she was working late at the *Oracle* office, putting the paper to bed. Jessica frowned as a new emotion overtook her— annoyance. Sometimes she didn't understand her sister at all! Hadn't Elizabeth noticed that Todd was seriously upset with her? How could she have been so wrapped up in her work that she dismissed the signals he'd given her in the cafeteria? And Jessica had come as close to spilling the whole story as she dared when she had warned her sister that boyfriends need to know their girlfriends care!

Of course, this wasn't the first time that Elizabeth had gotten so caught up in something that she ignored the people around her. Still, Elizabeth's dedication was usually to a good cause— like spreading information on sexual harassment. And at those times, Elizabeth always had the backing of Todd and all her friends. But this time was different. This time she was *hiding* the real reason she was spending time away from Todd. Naturally, he thought she was dating someone else!

What a mess, Jessica thought grimly. But she, of all people, understood how something could become so important to a person that all other things paled by comparison. Hadn't she gone a bit crazy when she and Elizabeth got the parts on

The Young and the Beautiful, and hadn't she left Sam in the dust as she gallivanted around Hollywood with Brandon Hunter? Hadn't she changed her whole personality when Adam Marvel came to town and convinced her to join the Good Friends cult? And when Bruce Patman had formed Club X and invited only boys to join, hadn't she been the only girl at Sweet Valley High to throw all of her good sense away to prove that she could meet any crazy dare Bruce devised? Before that episode was over she had found herself crossing a bridge in front of an oncoming train!

Elizabeth had made her see reason all of those times, and others as well. This time, Jessica had to make Elizabeth see reason—before it was too late. Before poor, neglected Todd took Shelley up on her offer of a relationship and Elizabeth was left with only her financial priorities and her journalistic pride.

Jessica shook her head to clear it. Poor Todd? What was she thinking? *Todd* was the one she should be blaming for this mess, not Elizabeth. Jessica's protective instincts surged forward. How dare he think Elizabeth was anything less than honest? By now he should *know*, without a doubt, that Elizabeth was the nicest, most generous person in the world.

Jessica gripped the steering wheel and swung around a corner. No doubt about it—Todd should have learned his lesson once and for all after the time he and Enid had suspected Elizabeth of blabbing their secrets all over school. *Jessica* had known that Elizabeth would never do something so awful. Jessica had set out to discover the truth, and when she had found out that Kris Lynch, a boy whom her sister had dated briefly, had stolen Elizabeth's diary and was spreading lies to get back at her for dumping him, she had set Todd and Enid straight.

Nope, Elizabeth would never lie to Todd. She might hold back some of the truth, but she would never deceive him maliciously. Jessica toyed with the idea of telling Todd the whole story, but then she thought better of it. Really, Todd didn't *deserve* the truth!

As Jessica drove into her driveway she had an idea—the first real idea she'd had since reading Todd's request. She'd take out all references to anything that might make Elizabeth suspicious. She'd let Elizabeth write the reply, but then later, after dinner, instead of just switching the envelopes, she'd write her own reply and substitute it for Elizabeth's letter. She already knew what she was going to say in her letter to Todd.

Dear Unbeliever, she would begin. *How can you even think about giving up on your girlfriend? She's been loyal and true to you for so long. Instead of jumping to conclusions, why don't you just be a little bit patient?*

Or something like that. She'd tell him to drop Shelley and patch things up with Elizabeth. *Or else*, she added silently.

A half-hour later, Jessica placed the rewritten-in-disguised-handwriting version of Todd's letter in the pile with all of the other requests for that day. No problem. She had everything under control.

The phone rang, and Jessica picked up the extension in her room, imagining it this time in shiny purple. "Hello?"

"Hi, Jess!"

"Sam! What do you think about purple and black for a new bedroom color scheme? Gosh, I feel like it's been forever since I've talked to you."

"It has. But I have a plan to solve that problem!"

Jessica lay down on her bed and propped her feet up on her headboard. "A plan, huh?" she teased. "Want to let me in on it?"

"Here's the scoop," Sam told her. "A friend of mine got tickets to tonight's Shining Steel concert."

"Ooh! Bill Lacey's band? I love their music!" Jessica said, sitting upright. "Lila tried to get tickets, but even with her father's connections, she couldn't. They were all sold out."

"Well, my friend can't go," Sam said, drawing out the suspense. "So . . . can you be ready in an hour? He gave the tickets to me!"

Jessica jumped off the bed and danced around, holding the receiver in one hand and the phone in the other. "We're going?" she shrieked. "Wait until I tell Lila. She'll just die!"

Sam laughed. "But can you be ready in an hour? I'll drive."

"I'll be ready in five minutes!" Jessica declared.

"See you in a few," Sam said. "I'll bring some food. And by the way . . ."

"Yes?" Jessica could hardly contain her excitement.

"I love purple."

Jessica was still dancing when she hung up the phone. What a surprise! And Lila really would be jealous. Jessica would be the envy of everyone at school who had tried to get a ticket and failed.

She looked at the clock. An hour wasn't much time. Jessica rushed around the room picking up outfits from the piles on her floor and discarding them. She hadn't seen Sam in a week and she wanted to look fabulous. Who knew? Maybe they'd get a chance to go backstage and meet the band. After all, she *did* know Bill Lacey, the famous rock star she'd met when she attended a party at his mansion with Brandon Hunter. Maybe she could pull some strings and get them even *more* tickets!

She finally selected a black stretch miniskirt and her new purple oversized sweater. Black enamel earrings completed her outfit. Then she used some hairspray to create a wild style. OK, so she looked pretty outrageous, but Shining Steel was a pretty outrageous band. Anyway, she had always liked purple and black as a color combination. Hadn't she wanted to buy a Jeep in those very colors? Jessica turned away from the mirror and looked around her room. Yes, it was definitely time to redecorate.

It wasn't until Jessica had called her mother to

let her know where she was going and sat down on her bed to wait for Sam that she remembered the letter she would have to write to Todd.

The doorbell rang just as she was reaching for some paper. "Coming!" she called down from the top of the stairs. *No problem,* she said confidently to herself. *I'll just get up early and do it in the morning before we go to the post office.*

Nine

As they drove up to the Wakefield house, Elizabeth and Enid passed Jessica and Sam in Sam's car.

"Thanks for the ride home," Elizabeth said when Enid pulled into the driveway. "Do you want to come in for a while?"

"No thanks," Enid said. "Hugh and I are going to the Shining Steel concert tonight, and I'm running late."

Elizabeth shrugged and got out of her friend's car. "OK. Have fun," she called as Enid drove off. Elizabeth continued up to the front door and went inside. That was when she saw Jessica's note. "So Jessica and Sam went to the concert, too," she said aloud. "I guess everyone is having fun but me!"

She couldn't really get mad at Jessica, though. Her note also said that the requests had been sorted and were stacked on her desk, ready to go. While Elizabeth had been at school working on the yearbook, Jessica had gone to the post office, sorted the mail, made notes on the margins of the more difficult letters, and logged all of the money into their bookkeeping ledger. That was at least two hours of work. Jessica had done her part; now Elizabeth had to do hers.

"May as well get to it," she said as she stared into the refrigerator a few minutes later. She took a casserole from the freezer and popped it into the microwave oven to defrost and reheat. By the time her parents arrived home, dinner would be ready. As soon as Elizabeth had programmed all of the buttons, she grabbed an apple and a glass of milk and climbed the stairs wearily to her room.

The letters were right on her desk, stacked neatly next to her computer, just as Jessica's note had said they would be. She took a bite of her apple, turned on the computer, and picked up the first letter.

Dear Letters R Us,

    I want to answer an ad in the personals section of the newspaper—enclosed is the ad—but I don't want to sound like a total bozo. Will you please write to this man and tell him I'm witty, charming, beautiful, talented, etc., and that I'm interested in going out on a friendly date? By the way, I'm a chef at The Good Earth.

Then Elizabeth read the ad: *Vegetarian organist, humorous and sincere, financially secure professional, nice, polite, easygoing, and romantic guy with a line-*

backer build, seeks fun-loving, intelligent female for walks, trips, spontaneous times, and quiet nights. It was signed *First Rate.*

"That should be easy," Elizabeth said, smiling to herself. Then she began to type.

Dear First,
If it's vegetarian cooking you're hooked on, you've come to the right place. Zucchini is my middle name. I'm a gourmet vegetarian chef with a penchant for organ music. I'd like to get together for a friendly date—mushrooms included.

Elizabeth printed the letter and started on the next one.

Dear Letters R Us,
I'm a freshman in college and I just moved away from home. My mother wants to know what I've been doing with my life for the past two months. Mainly she wants to know if I've found a girlfriend who will eventually marry me and give her grandchildren. Could you please write a letter for me telling her to mind her own business? I love her, but the pressure is driving me nuts.

An hour later Elizabeth had answered six letters. She was beginning to think that she might actually get done early that night and have a chance to call Todd. She had promised she would. She wondered briefly if Jessica had been right when she had said she thought Todd was *really* upset with her. She hoped not.

She reached for the next letter and read it. "That poor boy," she said, propping the letter up against the computer. He was torn between his steady girlfriend, who was obviously not paying any attention to him, and a perfectly nice girl who cared a lot about him. Elizabeth was glad that the letter she had written for the other girl to send to him had worked. She loved playing matchmaker! Hadn't she done a wonderful job getting Enid and Hugh back together? And hadn't she been instrumental in getting Sam and Jessica back together after the Brandon Hunter episode?

Elizabeth's stomach growled loudly. *Oops*, she thought. *I'd better eat dinner before I start matchmaking.* Elizabeth went downstairs and joined her parents for a generous helping of the piping-hot enchilada casserole. When they had finished their after-dinner coffee, she marched back upstairs to finish working.

Elizabeth sat down at the computer, thought for a moment, and then began to write. First, the letter to the new girl. *Dear _____, I really loved your letter. It was the best letter I've ever received.*

Elizabeth smiled. She figured she might as well compliment herself. After all, it *was* a great letter she had written. Warm, intelligent . . .

Up until now, I never realized that you felt this way about me, Elizabeth wrote on. *I guess you can be friends with someone for a long time and never see them for who they really are. I'm glad you took the risk and wrote to me. Most girls would be too scared to tell a boy their feelings. I really admire you for your courage.*

Will you go out with me on Friday night? I'd like to have the chance to get to know you better and explore what might be the beginning of a wonderful new relationship.

Elizabeth looked at the letter critically. Was it too gushy? Was it too impersonal? No, it was just right. It didn't specifically promise anything; it merely hinted at future possibilities. She hoped the girl wouldn't be too shy to respond.

"Now for the letter to his girlfriend," Elizabeth said, narrowing her eyes. Any girl who would ignore someone as great as this guy obviously was—tender and caring, a real sweetheart—deserved to be shaken up a bit. *This guy sounds a lot like Todd*, she thought. *And anyone who wouldn't appreciate a guy like Todd*, Elizabeth decided, *deserves the single life.*

Dear _____,   Lately I've noticed that I'm pretty low on your priority list, she typed. *You're always too busy to see me and you aren't honest enough to tell me why. Well, whatever you're doing and whomever you're doing it with have come first for the last time. I think we should cool it for a while, date other people. If you decide you'd like to speak to me about this, give me a call—if you can spare the time!*

When Elizabeth finished the letter, she had a feeling of great satisfaction. As she looked over the remaining requests in the stack, her thoughts were on the boy and girl whom she had helped so much already. For the first time, she wished that their letter-writing service wasn't so anonymous. Wouldn't it be fun to actually *meet* this couple-to-be and share in their happiness?

Elizabeth got up from the computer and went into Jessica's room to look for the envelopes in which the letters had come. But her twin's room was such a disaster that even after extensive searching, Elizabeth concluded that the use of a bulldozer wouldn't have helped. Well, she would talk to Jessica first thing in the morning, get the return addresses from the envelopes, and mail the new letters in the afternoon. Their turnaround time was getting faster and faster.

It was already ten o'clock when Elizabeth finally wandered downstairs to rustle up some apple pie and to say good night to her parents. Briefly, she thought about calling Todd before she went to bed, but then she decided it was too late.

"How is that letter-writing service going?" her father asked. "We haven't seen much of you two lately."

Elizabeth smiled tiredly and flopped down on the sofa. "Actually, it's going better than either of us ever dreamed. I estimate that about one week more will do it. We'll have achieved our lofty financial goals!"

"That's wonderful, Elizabeth," Mrs. Wakefield said. "But what about the service after that? Are you going to keep it going?"

"Well, it's been incredibly lucrative, but Jessica and I both feel that the letter-writing business takes too much time away from the other things we have to do, like homework and seeing our friends. We know we need to slow down." Elizabeth folded her arms across her chest. "The trouble is, quite a few people are counting on the service. I mean, in some cases, we've received several requests from the same person. I'd hate to let our best clients down." Elizabeth laughed wearily. "Do you have any ideas?"

"Well," Mr. Wakefield began, "there *are* a couple of ways you could slow down without quitting entirely. How about hiring other people to help?"

"That's one idea. We thought we might ask Enid and a couple of the girls who write for *The Oracle* to help, if we decide to go that route," Elizabeth said, taking a bite of her apple pie. "Another idea would be to advertise a slower turnaround time, say two weeks instead of one."

"Or you could charge more per letter," her mother suggested. "That would cut down on your customers."

Elizabeth put her empty plate on the coffee table. "I'm not sure *what* we're going to do," she said. She picked up the U.S. Sports catalog lying next to her plate and flipped automatically to the advertisement for the warmup jacket she had ordered for Todd. It was due to arrive any day now, and then she could finally tell him what had been keeping her so busy. But for some reason, Elizabeth felt melancholy. She glanced quickly at her parents, contentedly sharing an evening together just reading and talking, and she thought about how little she had seen Todd during the past weeks. Somehow, her plan didn't seem worth it anymore. "Right now," she said, surprising herself with the firmness of her tone, "I'm ready to quit altogether."

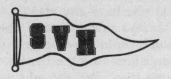

Ten

"Are you in there, Jess? Ready to go?" Elizabeth called into her twin's room the next morning.

Jessica opened her eyes and stared at the bright sunlight streaming in her window. "Oh, no!" she grumbled. "I overslept!" She tried to throw her legs over the side of the bed, got tangled in her sheets, and landed on the floor in a heap.

"Are you all right?" Elizabeth asked, opening the door. She grinned at Jessica's disheveled appearance. "I'm leaving in ten minutes. Where are the return addresses for the last batch of letters? I finished writing the responses last night."

Oh, no, Jessica thought again. She hadn't gotten up early enough to rewrite the letter to Todd! She tore at her sheets and finally managed to escape their cotton clutches.

"There! I'm up," she announced as she ran a hand through her tangled hair. "The concert was fantastic, but we didn't get home until after midnight," Jessica told Elizabeth as she rummaged through several piles of clothing for something clean to wear. She was also stalling for time. She couldn't just hand the addresses over to her sister. *That* would be an even bigger disaster than having to write Todd's letter in study hall.

That was it! Jessica smiled as she pulled on a pair of jeans and tucked in her new hand-painted denim blouse, which she had unearthed from beneath her chair. She would rewrite Todd's letter in study hall and mail the letters after school.

"Was there a big crowd at the concert?" Elizabeth asked.

Jessica ran a brush through her hair and rushed to the bathroom to wash her face and brush her teeth. Through a mouthful of toothpaste she told Elizabeth about the evening.

"Sold out. You wouldn't believe it! I think everyone in Sweet Valley was there. Well, except those who didn't stand in line for seventeen hours to buy tickets. I saw Enid and Hugh."

"I wondered if you would," Elizabeth commented as she checked her watch. "But about those addresses—"

"Sam was so prepared," Jessica inserted neatly. "He brought food and soda, and we had our own little party while everyone else wasted time out in the lobby buying refreshments."

"Good thinking. Are you ready now?" Elizabeth glanced again at her watch. "We have just enough time to address the envelopes and drop by the post office to make the morning mail."

Didn't she ever give up? Jessica thought fast. "What's the hurry? I thought that since we're running late I'd just address them in study hall and mail them after school."

"That's ridiculous, Jess," Elizabeth countered. "We have time right now. And I don't want to lose an entire day on this batch. Look, I'll address the envelopes while you go grab something for breakfast."

"Uh, no, Liz, really, it's all right," Jessica protested. "After all, I skipped out on you last night. I'll take care of everything and meet you downstairs in a few minutes."

But Elizabeth seemed not to have heard her sister. She didn't budge. Instead, she sat on Jessica's rumpled bed and asked more questions about the concert. What had the group been wearing? What songs had they played? Anything new? How was the crowd? Had she seen anyone from Sweet Valley High there besides Enid?

Finally, Jessica realized that Elizabeth wasn't going to leave the room without her. She couldn't stall any longer. Reluctantly, she sat down to address the clean envelopes and insert the letters Elizabeth had written. She made sure that the envelope that contained Todd's letters was tucked in the middle of the stack. Elizabeth had an eagle eye, but there was still a chance that on the way to the post office Jessica could slip Todd's letter out of the stack undetected, rewrite it, and mail it later.

"OK. Let's go," Jessica said cheerily. "I'll tell you more about the concert on the way to the post office and school. By the way, did I mention that my knowing Bill Lacey got us an invitation backstage?"

"No. Really? That's fantastic!" Elizabeth cried.

The girls left the room and headed downstairs.

"Actually, the most fantastic part of the whole thing is that I came across a great idea for my room—a chrome daybed. Bill said he ordered his from the Sears catalog, just like a regular person! I think I'll make the daybed the focal point of the room and then get a bunch of purple and lavender pillows to throw around on top of it for that casually elegant look."

"That's just what you need in your room, Jess," Elizabeth said with a chuckle. "A few more pillows to throw around."

Jessica put her hand to her chest. "You underestimate me, Elizabeth. I'm turning over a new leaf. I'm going to clean up *everything* before I paint. The walls are going to be purple, you know. And I'm going to buy a purple velvet quilt. There'll be a place for everything, and everything will be in its place. It's fine for me to throw things around in the Hershey Bar, but purple is too *sophisticated* for clutter."

Elizabeth rolled her eyes. "I can't wait to see this," she remarked as they entered the kitchen together. "When do you plan to start?"

"As soon as we wrap up the letter-writing service. And as soon as I pay for the portable CD player and my dress at Lisette's and Sam's racing gloves!"

Jessica grabbed a container of yogurt from the

refrigerator, holding tight all the while to the stack of letters. All she had to do was keep the letters clutched in her *own* hand, jump out of the Jeep before Elizabeth had a chance to when they reached the post office, and mail the letters herself. Elizabeth would never know that she hadn't mailed the envelope addressed to Todd.

But her plan was foiled the moment they stepped out of the front door.

"Hello, Mr. Ramsey," Elizabeth called to the mailman coming up their walk.

"Oh, no! Just my luck. The mailman is early," Jessica mumbled.

"Did you say something, Jess?" Elizabeth asked.

"Nothing worth repeating," Jessica replied.

"Here you go," Elizabeth said, tugging the letters out of Jessica's grip. "This saves us a lot of time," she added, smiling at him.

Jessica stood silently and watched her hopes disappear into the mailman's sack. What was she going to do now? All of her pleasantly purple thoughts fled.

"So, Liz," she began as soon as her sister turned the ignition key and started the engine. "How did the letter-writing go last night? There were some pretty *interesting* requests in the batch, don't you think?"

"Especially the one from that boy who wants to dump his unappreciative girlfriend for the girl he's been friends with—you know, the one who has a crush on him. I feel like such a matchmaker," Elizabeth said happily. "I think those two were really meant for each other."

"How can you say that?" Jessica asked, trying to fight down the sick feeling in her stomach.

"Oh, it's just a hunch. Besides, his girlfriend doesn't deserve him. She never pays any attention to him."

Jessica put her hand to her head. Now she felt dizzy. She hated to ask the next question, but she knew she had to. "What exactly did you say in your letters? I mean, I, uh, hope you didn't go overboard."

"Nope. I only wrote what the guy wanted me to write. Let's see if I can remember some of it." Elizabeth was silent for a moment, and then she began to recap the letters.

" ' . . . I guess you can be friends with someone for a long time and never see them for who they really are. I'm glad you took the risk and wrote to me . . . I really admire you for your courage. Will you go out with me on Friday night? . . . explore what might be the beginning of a wonderful new relationship.' "

"You didn't!" Jessica cried in horror. "Oh, Liz, that was really too much. They barely *know* each other. Don't you think you're pushing things too hard, rushing things?"

"Someone has to," Elizabeth replied blithely. "Wait until you hear what I wrote to his wayward girlfriend."

Jessica leaned her head against the Jeep's window. "I can't wait."

95

"I had the guy say that it was obvious he was low on her priority list and that it was too bad she was too busy for him and not honest enough to tell him why."

It was worse than Jessica could have imagined. Elizabeth was digging a large hole and throwing herself—and her relationship—in headfirst. Jessica knew she was going to have to do something drastic, because there was absolutely no way that she could let Todd receive those letters.

She looked over at her sister, who was so proud of the way she had solved the "unknown" couple's problems. Jessica shook her head and slumped down in the seat, unaware of the warm morning breeze or the crash of the ocean waves in the distance. All she could think of was how Elizabeth was going to kill her when she found out what was really going on. It was inevitable that she *would* find out. And if Jessica didn't do something pretty amazing pretty fast, Elizabeth would find out through the mail!

That afternoon, Elizabeth met Todd outside of his last class. She hadn't seen him all day because she'd been so busy, but she was determined to spare an hour or so from her hectic schedule for him.

"Want to go to the Dairi Burger and hang out for a while?" Elizabeth asked.

"You're kidding," Todd exclaimed. "You have a few minutes for little old me?"

Elizabeth laughed, ignoring the sarcasm. "It hasn't been *that* bad, has it?"

"Worse," Todd informed her.

"Well, I'll make it up to you this afternoon. I'll buy the shakes," she offered.

"Actually," Todd said as they walked to his locker to collect his books, "I thought I'd go watch the girls' basketball team practice. Uh, Shelley asked me to check out her rebounding. She wants to bring her average up."

"That sounds OK to me. I'll go with you," Elizabeth said, shifting her backpack to her other shoulder and reaching for Todd's hand.

They walked in silence to the gym. But that was just fine with Elizabeth. She was glad simply to be with Todd. She glanced over at him, but his thoughts seemed to be elsewhere. And that was fine, too. So was the fact that his hand wasn't grasping hers as firmly as usual. They had been going steady for a long time. They didn't have to keep up a constant flow of chatter. They didn't have to be romantic all the time. They understood each other.

As they climbed the bleachers Elizabeth imagined what Todd would look like in the navy-blue and gold warmup jacket. It would go nicely with his dark brown hair and his coffee-colored eyes. Elizabeth felt her face grow flushed and her eyes grow moist. How she had missed being with Todd these past few weeks! She could hardly wait to see the look on his face when he found out that she had been spending all of her time earning money to buy him a special gift!

Elizabeth's good mood was not meant to last. As soon as they sat down Todd turned to her and raised one questioning eyebrow. "So tell me, to what do I owe this honor today? Did you run out of better things to do?"

"No," Elizabeth said, frowning a little at his tone. "I—I just managed to catch up for a while and thought I deserved a break."

"Is Jessica taking a break, too? Or is she hard at work on whatever it is you two are supposed to be doing while *you* play this time?"

Elizabeth's face flushed again, only this time it was with hurt—and anger.

"What are you talking about, Todd? You're acting so strange."

"*I'm* acting strange? That's pretty funny coming from you. Take last night, for example. First you told me that you and Jessica would be busy working on your project again. And then you said you would call me. Well, you never called me, and this morning I heard that Jessica was out with Sam at the Shining Steel concert. How do I know you weren't there, too? Your 'I'm swamped' line is beginning to sound pretty lame."

For a moment, Elizabeth couldn't speak. And when she found her voice, it came out sounding odd and distant, like the voice of someone who'd just experienced a very bad shock.

"How can you say that?" she asked. "How can you accuse me of . . . I spent all evening at home writing let—"

"Why should I believe you, Liz?" Todd demanded. "You never called me. And you lied to me about you and Jessica working on some project *together*."

Elizabeth's mouth dropped open in disbelief. "What exactly are you accusing me of, Todd?" she asked.

"I'm accusing you of not telling me the truth. C'mon, Elizabeth. Let's have it! Once and for all, why are you sneaking around and keeping whatever it is you're doing a secret from me? Who is he?"

Elizabeth sat up straighter. This was absolutely ridiculous. One minute she was holding Todd's hand and thinking about how happy he would be when she presented him with her gift, and the next minute he was accusing her of two-timing him! She was getting angrier by the minute.

She scooted farther away on the bench and glared at him. "I am *not* sneaking around and I am *not* hiding anything. At least, not what you *think* I'm hiding. I told you that what I was doing was a surprise for you. Can't you let it go at that? Can't you believe me?"

Todd glared back. "I guess I can't," he said. "But if you won't tell me what you're doing, then I suppose there's nothing I can do about it. Let's just drop it, OK?" He turned away from her then and watched Shelley and the rest of the girls' team on the court.

He didn't take his eyes off them when Elizabeth said that it was OK with her, too.

Elizabeth sat beside him watching the court as well, but with unseeing eyes. She was miserable. What was going on? How had things between her and Todd gotten so awful—and without her knowing about it? Sure, she had known that Todd was upset about the dates she had broken. And sure, Jessica had tried to tell her that she wasn't paying enough attention to Todd lately, but . . . Elizabeth squirmed in her seat. And then she took a deep breath. "I saw the pictures that Jim took of you at one of the games. Whizzer Wilkins will be on the front page of the sports section of the yearbook," she said. "What do you think of that? You're a celebrity."

"Swell."

Elizabeth took another breath and tried again. "I saw the layout for the next issue of *Visions* today. Olivia had Rod Sullivan do a fantastic graphic design for the cover. It looks almost three-dimensional. He's really talented, don't you think?"

"Uh-huh."

"My mom asked when you're coming over for dinner again," Elizabeth said, desperate for some heartfelt response—or at least for a reply longer than one word.

"I'll have to let you know," Todd said, his eyes still riveted on the court. And Shelley.

Elizabeth watched her, too. Shelley was grace personified on the basketball court. "Poetry in Motion," the title of the photograph that Shelley's boyfriend, Jim, had submitted to the *Sweet Valley News* and won a prize for, really was an apt description of the fluidity with which she played. Elizabeth couldn't see anything wrong with her rebounds, or for that matter, with anything else she did.

But Todd was studying every move she made with unshakable concentration.

"Have you talked to Shelley any more since last Saturday?" she finally asked. "I saw Jim in the photo lab, but he seemed as preoccupied as usual."

"Yeah, we've talked a couple of times," Todd said.

"About what?"

"Stuff."

Suddenly, Elizabeth was fed up with Todd's lack of communication. If she didn't know better, she would think that *he* was hiding something from her. "What kind of stuff?" Elizabeth asked.

"Um, just basketball stuff. You know, the usual."

Elizabeth shook her head. She couldn't take another moment of this. She was beginning to feel like a yo-yo of emotions. Besides, she probably had a pile of letters waiting for her at home. Jessica was supposed to have gone to the post office after school.

Elizabeth stood up to leave. Todd didn't even appear to notice. *I'll be glad when this is over*, she thought tiredly. She was mad at herself for her stupid pride, which wouldn't let her tell him the truth about the letter-writing service. And she was mad at Todd for trying to make her feel guilty and then ignoring her.

"I'll see you later," Elizabeth said.

"Do you need a ride home?" Todd asked, his eyes briefly directed toward her. Elizabeth could tell by the tone of his voice that he had asked only out of obligation, not out of desire.

She tried to keep her tone light in what was a vain effort to hide the fact that she was hurt by his chilly attitude.

"No, thanks," she said. "I'm sure Enid is still around somewhere."

It was the first time in a long time that Todd didn't kiss her goodbye.

Eleven

It was Friday morning, and Jessica was waiting outside Todd's house. She had taken care to fix her hair back in a ponytail and dress like Elizabeth in what was a pretty conservative outfit for Jessica—jeans and a lightweight pink sweater. If her plan worked, she would change clothes before she went to school so that Elizabeth wouldn't suspect she had been pretending to be her.

"If only I can catch Todd's mailman and convince him to give me that letter before Todd sees it, before Elizabeth's relationship *totally* falls apart," she whispered aloud.

Jessica leaned her arms on the Jeep's steering wheel and stared down the street in the direction she assumed the mailman would come. Then she thought about the change that had come over her twin the afternoon before, when she'd had her fight with Todd.

Elizabeth had told Jessica everything—the way Todd suspected that she was two-timing him, the way he had accused her of having gone to the concert with someone else, and then the way she had refused to enlighten him about the real reason she had been so busy lately. *It's an impossible situation,* Jessica thought grimly. *And I'm the only one who knows the whole story.* She couldn't even really be mad at Todd anymore for not trusting her sister. Now she felt sorry for him. What was he supposed to think was going on?

Even if Elizabeth hadn't told Jessica the whole story, she would have known that something was very wrong between her sister and Todd. Elizabeth was obviously depressed. She had gone through the motions of doing homework and writing letters without any of her usual enthusiasm. Jessica hadn't even been able to perk her up by telling her about the latest hot gossip at school, and there had been some pretty juicy tidbits—like Annie Whitman and Tony Esteban being on the outs and Jennifer Mitchell and John Pfeifer not far behind.

Jessica closed her eyes for a second. She hoped she wasn't too late to turn this whole fiasco around. She didn't want Todd and Elizabeth becoming just another breakup statistic. Suddenly her ears detected the sound of another vehicle driving slowly down the street. It sounded just like her Jeep, she was sure of it. Her eyes snapped open in time to see the mailman parking a few doors away from Todd's house. Suddenly, she smiled with recognition. The Wilkinses had the same mailman on Country Club Drive as the Wakefields had on Calico Drive.

This should be easy, Jessica said to herself as she climbed out of the Jeep. *He already knows me. More importantly, he already knows Elizabeth.*

"Mr. Ramsey!" Jessica hailed him as he started up the walkway to the Wilkinses' front door. As she got closer to him she noticed a familiar-looking envelope protruding from the bundle in his hand. "Excuse me, Mr. Ramsey?"

"Why, hello, Elizabeth," Mr. Ramsey responded. He looked around, pretending to be confused. "I'm not on the wrong street, am I?"

Works every time, Jessica thought.

"No," she said with a smile. "Mr. Ramsey, I have a problem and I'm hoping you can help me with it. I've been waiting here for half an hour hoping to catch you."

"Well, I hope I can be of service. What can I do for you?" Mr. Ramsey continued his direct course toward the Wilkinses' door.

Jessica stepped in front of him before he reached the stairs to the porch. "Well, um . . . it's about a letter that you have in your hand there," she said, pointing to the offending missive, her eyes welling with unshed tears. "There's been a terrible mistake! I wrote my boyfriend, Todd Wilkins, a letter breaking up with him, and now I've changed my mind. That's the letter right there." Jessica pointed again, then turned her hand palm up, waiting for him to hand it over. When he didn't, she looked up into his face.

He wasn't smiling now. "And?" Mr. Ramsey prompted.

"And . . . I was hoping you would give it back to me before Todd sees it."

"I'm sorry, Elizabeth," Mr. Ramsey said. "I'm quite surprised, actually, that you would ask me to do such a thing. Tampering with the mail is against the law."

"But *I* wrote the letter," Jessica cried. "Isn't it my property?"

"Not once you put a stamp on it and send it. I could get in big trouble if I didn't deliver this, or any other letter for that matter."

"But if Todd gets it . . . well . . ." Jessica wailed, "it's just going to ruin my life, that's all!"

Mr. Ramsey shook his head. "I sympathize, Elizabeth. I really do. I know that the course of young love doesn't always run smoothly. I raised three daughters myself and believe me, life with them was a roller-coaster ride I won't soon forget. I'm sure you'll be able to explain to your young man that writing the letter was a mistake. If he loves you, he'll understand. If he doesn't understand, then maybe he wasn't the boy for you after all."

Jessica didn't want romantic advice. She wanted action! But she knew better than to plead her case any more with Mr. Ramsey. For one thing, the law was the law. For another, Elizabeth Wakefield wouldn't make a scene. Jessica sighed. Elizabeth wouldn't even be in this predicament in the first place if it weren't for her twin sister.

"I suppose you're right, Mr. Ramsey," Jessica said sadly as she watched her last hope slip silently into the mail slot on Todd's door. "I know you can't break the law. I don't know . . . maybe talking things out with Todd *will* help."

"That's the spirit, Elizabeth," the mail carrier said brightly. "Maybe sending this letter will get your boyfriend's attention, and maybe you'll wind up closer than ever before."

"I hope you're right." Jessica smiled sadly and turned toward the Jeep. "For right now, what's done is done," she added quietly.

And that's what Jessica kept telling herself on the drive to school and while she stopped briefly at a gas station to change back into her own clothes. She had done everything she could to stop the letters. Maybe it was fate. Maybe Todd and Elizabeth *would* see the letters as a sort of turning point, and maybe their relationship would improve because of them. Better yet, maybe Todd would read the letters Elizabeth had written for him and decide that he didn't want to go through with sending them after all. She couldn't really imagine Todd breaking up with Elizabeth and dating Shelley. Still, stranger things had happened.

Jessica squirmed behind the steering wheel. "Besides, it's all Liz's fault for writing such good letters!" she remarked to no one in particular. If Elizabeth hadn't insisted on making Shelley's letter so romantic in the first place, then Todd wouldn't ever have gotten interested in her. And if she hadn't taken the liberty of writing a wonderful response from Todd to Shelley and, to top it all off, another letter breaking up with herself, none of them would be in this mess.

Yes, it was really mostly Elizabeth's fault. Jessica stopped at a red light and tapped the steering wheel impatiently. If only Elizabeth had let Jessica do her part of the job by mailing the letters, then those fabulously written but deadly letters wouldn't be on the floor of Todd's entry hall at that very minute, waiting to explode.

The light turned green and Jessica hit the gas. Yes, she decided, Elizabeth was largely to blame. She tried not to think about the fact that she, Jessica, could have stopped the whole mess early on by telling Elizabeth the truth, or by confronting Shelley or Todd, or by destroying the letters and returning the money.

Jessica parked in the Sweet Valley High parking lot, turned off the Jeep, and rubbed the bridge of her nose. She would much rather worry about which shade of purple to paint her walls than about her sister's life, which was about to be ruined.

"Please, Todd," she whispered to the wind. "Don't mail those letters!"

"I don't know what to do," Elizabeth confessed to Enid over lunch. "Todd is acting so strange lately." She held up her thumb and forefinger a fraction of an inch apart. "He came *this* close to accusing me of going out with someone else behind his back."

"That's just plain ridiculous," Enid protested. "What would give him that idea?"

"Well, I *have* been pretty busy lately. Jessica and

108

I started a little business a couple of weeks ago, and it's been taking up a lot of my time."

"So that's why I haven't seen you around much," Enid exclaimed. "What business? Why didn't you tell me?"

"We were trying to keep it all confidential, but I can't see the point in that anymore. Anyway, I know you can keep a secret. Jessica and I are the Letters R Us letter-writing service."

"You're kidding!" Enid laughed. "Those posters all over town and at school—they're yours? It's a really good idea, Liz. It's going well, huh?"

"*Too* well," Elizabeth admitted. "We've just been *too* busy. And that's what caused the problem with Todd. He's been feeling left out."

"But doesn't he know about the business?" Enid asked.

Elizabeth grimaced. "No. That's the ironic part. I got into the letter-writing business because I needed the money to buy Todd a present, an incredible warmup jacket that I ordered from U.S. Sports. Anyway, I decided not to tell him what I was doing because I didn't want to spoil the surprise," Elizabeth explained. "At first it was kind of a joke between us. I'd tease him and tell him that I was working on something that would be for his own good in the long run, and he'd try to get me to slip up and spill the real story."

"And now?" Enid asked, leaning toward her friend, her eyes clearly showing her concern.

"And now it's not a joke anymore. When Todd started pressuring me to tell him the truth—saying he had a right to know what I was doing—I got really angry. I mean, if he can't trust me enough to believe me when I say I'm tied up with a project, then what kind of a relationship do we have?"

Enid bit her lip thoughtfully. "No offense, Liz, but it seems to me that your pride is getting in the way of your common sense," she remarked. "Why don't you just level with him? I mean, the jacket won't be a surprise anymore, but at least you two will be on good terms again."

Elizabeth sighed and took a sip of her orange juice. "I don't know if we *can* be on good terms again. He really hurt my feelings when he chose to stay and watch the girls' basketball team practice instead of going to the Dairi Burger with me. I'm slaving away, trying to do something nice for him, and he repays me by doubting me, then ignoring me."

"I guess you could say there are two sides to this issue," Enid argued. "The trouble is, Todd doesn't know *yours*. All he sees is his side because you won't *let* him see yours. Why don't you just talk to him, let him know that it's all a big misunderstanding?"

Elizabeth smiled. "You're a good friend, Enid."

"You've been there for me plenty of times— when I was having problems with George, and then with Hugh. I've had to wrestle with my pride more than once!"

"And you're glad now that you did?" Elizabeth asked.

"Of course. Hugh and I wouldn't be together

today if you hadn't convinced me to talk honestly to him about how I was feeling," Enid admitted. "You gave me valuable advice. It's only fair that I give the same advice back to you."

Elizabeth smiled ruefully. "I guess I'd rather Todd came to me. I still think he's the one who needs to apologize."

Enid groaned. "But Liz! Right now he doesn't think he has anything to apologize for! He thinks *you're* the one doing the ignoring. And let's face it—he's right." Enid laid a hand on her friend's arm. "Talk to him, Liz. He's worth it."

"I'll think about it," Elizabeth said. "Seriously. As soon as Jessica and I are done with this week's letters."

Enid sat back and sighed. "If I were you, I wouldn't wait that long."

Twelve

Later that evening, Jessica was receiving much the same advice from Sam.

"I think you should tell her the whole story," Sam said.

They had driven out to the beach, and Jessica had just finished explaining the situation to Sam. "I don't see how you can say that," Jessica moaned. "What if Todd decides *not* to mail the letters? Then I'll have upset Liz for nothing."

"But what if he *does* mail them? Elizabeth will be devastated!" Sam said. "Wouldn't you want to know if you were in her situation?"

"Sam, I *can't* tell her!" Jessica cried. "I'm always doing devious things behind her back, and she'll accuse me of plotting against her or something! And the truth is, the last thing I wanted to do was to hurt her!"

"Elizabeth won't accuse you of anything. She

isn't like that at all. She's been more than fair to you every time you've gotten yourself into a mess. Look how she came through for you when you fell head over heels in love with Brandon Hunter—and don't tell me you didn't," Sam said, putting up a hand to stop her protest. "When your personality changed overnight and you became a celebrity, Elizabeth stood by you and helped us get back together. And may I remind you she did all that *after* you sneakily plotted to get her to audition for the show, against her will?"

"That was totally different," Jessica argued. "That whole scheme was for *my* own good. *I* wanted to be a star. I acted selfishly and I deserved to get into trouble. But this time I had *Elizabeth's* best interest in mind. This time I was trying to save her the heartache of knowing about the letters. It was all for *her* own good."

"And I'm sure she'll understand that. She's your sister and she knows you love her more than anyone else," Sam encouraged.

Jessica twisted her toes in the sand and gazed out at the sunset. Orange and fuchsia tilted crazily into a bank of gray clouds on the horizon. "Liz has a big thing about being honest. She'll be mad that I didn't level with her the minute I got Shelley's first letter."

"You won't know that until you tell her."

"I'll think about it, OK?"

Sam stood and pulled Jessica up with him. He spun her around and set her down with a resounding kiss. "While you're thinking about it, why don't we stop by Guido's Pizza Palace for a large pepperoni-and-mushroom? I have a sudden craving for junk food."

Jessica punched him playfully on the arm. "A man after my own heart." Sam put his arm around her, and together they strolled back to the Jeep.

Jessica tried to put all thoughts of Elizabeth and Todd from her mind as she and Sam drove to Guido's. Besides, it wasn't going to be long before she and Elizabeth could quit the letter-writing business for good. She tapped her free foot to the beat of the song playing on the standard radio in her Jeep, and imagined how much better it would sound as soon as she installed the deluxe AM/FM radio and CD player.

And Sam would be thrilled when he saw his new racing gloves. Yes, she thought, things might still turn out splendidly. Somehow.

"Hey, some of the group from your school is still here," Sam said as they entered Guido's a few minutes later.

They sat down in a booth, and Jessica scanned the interior of the restaurant. "It looks as if the basketball teams came here after the game," she commented. "Yep. I see Todd over there."

"We should go over and ask who won," Sam suggested.

Jessica was just about to get Todd's attention when she noticed who he was talking to. Shelley. Their heads were bent together, and Shelley was giggling.

"See what I mean?" Jessica nudged Sam and

jerked her head in Todd and Shelley's direction. "They're getting closer all the time. Poor Liz."

Sam turned to study the couple, then turned back and shook his head. "I think they're just two friends getting together after a game, Jess. They aren't here alone. They're with a group. The basketball teams at Sweet Valley High support each other, remember?"

"They may have *come* with the group," Jessica observed wryly, "but they're *here* with each other. You'll just have to trust me on this, Sam. I've seen people isolate themselves in a crowd before. You and I have done it often enough."

The waitress came to their table and took their order. When she was gone, Jessica resumed staring at Todd and Shelley over Sam's shoulder.

"Give it a rest, Jess," Sam pleaded. "There's nothing you can do about it right now."

"I could go over there and pretend to be Liz. That would shake Shelley up!"

"You're being overly dramatic," Sam said. "Besides, Todd would recognize you in a second."

Jessica sighed and looked at Sam. "I *have* to do *something!*"

Sam took Jessica's hand and squeezed it. "What you really have to do is tell Elizabeth the truth."

"As soon as I figure out the best time," Jessica said, looking past Sam again.

"The sooner the better," Sam urged. "Now, let's talk about something else. What's this about redecorating your room in purple? I was just getting used to chocolate brown."

Reluctantly, Jessica allowed herself to be led

away from the subject of Todd and Shelley, but she couldn't stop watching them as they ate their pizza.

"Did you check out the Sears catalog for the chrome daybed?" Sam asked.

"Yes, and the daybed like the one we saw in Bill Lacey's dressing room isn't very expensive," Jessica said. "And if I make a bunch of purple pillows instead of buying them, I think I can afford to do the whole room at once—paint, bed, and accessories."

"Isn't all purple going to be boring?"

Jessica took a bite of her pizza and let the cheese stretch out. "I might make some black pillows just for contrast. And of course a few metallic silver ones. What do you think they're talking about over there, Sam? Shouldn't they be talking to other people, too?"

Sam shook his head. "You're impossible! Let's take the rest of the pizza and get out of here before you do something you'll regret."

Three days later, Elizabeth arrived home without Jessica. Her twin had to stay after school for cheerleading practice. Lila was going to wait for her and bring her home.

Elizabeth turned the key in the lock and entered the empty house.

"I'm tired of being alone," she said, her voice echoing in the entryway. Todd hadn't spoken to her since Thursday, and she had just spent the first weekend in a very long time without him. It seemed that everywhere she looked, *other* people were cozily paired up. Jessica was happily going out with Sam, Enid with Hugh, her parents with each other. She felt as if she were the only person in all of Sweet Valley without a partner.

Steven would be a welcome sight right now, she thought. She decided she'd call him and ask his advice, right after she read the mail.

She reached down to retrieve it from the floor and immediately noticed a letter from Todd.

"What in the world?" she asked as she ripped open the envelope.

The letter had been printed on computer paper. She began to read.

Dear Liz,

Lately I've noticed that I'm pretty low on your priority list. You're always too busy to see me and you aren't honest enough to tell me why. Well, whatever you're doing and whomever you're doing it with have come first for the last time. I think we should cool it for a while, date other people. If you decide you'd like to speak to me about this, give me a call—if you can spare the time.

Elizabeth's eyes opened wide, and the letter fell from her nerveless fingers. She couldn't believe it. There had to be some mistake. The mailman must have sent the letter back for insufficient postage.

But that couldn't be, she realized, because Letters R Us used a post office box as a return address. She picked up the envelope and stared at Todd's distinctive handwriting, then looked again at the letter where he had inserted her name in the blank spot after *Dear*. He hadn't even bothered to copy it over! He'd just written her name in, as if he were sending a form letter!

Elizabeth paced furiously. How could this have happened? *Why* had this happened? Suddenly she stood stock still and then began to shake all over.

"If Todd sent me *this* letter," she said, "then . . . then . . . he sent the *other* letter to someone else . . . someone who is madly in love with *my* boyfriend!"

Elizabeth kicked her backpack across the hall and strode to the kitchen. She yanked open the refrigerator and pulled out the pitcher of orange juice. Taking off the lid, she took a long drink directly from the container and then slammed it down on the table. Then she took out the cake left over from dessert the night before, grabbed a fork, and began to eat in great bites.

"Why? Why? Why?" she asked herself. "*Why* didn't I recognize Todd's handwriting on the request letter? Who is the other girl? She signed her name Blythe. Why don't I *know* her?"

She held her fork in the air and waved a huge piece of cake at her imaginary rival. "Someone changed the handwriting and the details of those letters so that I wouldn't know what was going on. And that someone could only be—"

The front door slammed.

"*Jessica!*" Elizabeth yelled. "Get in here this instant! You have some *major* explaining to do!"

"What is it?" Jessica asked frantically as she ran into the kitchen. "I saw your backpack on the

118

floor and you're . . ." She gaped at Elizabeth. "You're eating the *whole* cake?"

Elizabeth looked at the plate, where only a small piece remained of what had been almost half a cake. Her eyes narrowed, and she shook her fork at Jessica. "I received a very interesting letter in the mail today," she said through gritted teeth. "A very *familiar* letter. In fact, I wrote it myself."

Jessica sank down in a chair and watched her sister chug-a-lug some juice. She buried her face in her hands.

"I wanted to tell you, Liz. I promised Sam I'd tell you, but the time never seemed to be right. I was hoping Todd wouldn't send the letter."

"Wouldn't send the letter? Hah!" Elizabeth downed another bite of cake. "You knew about this all along and chose not to tell me! You *lied* to me! You rewrote the letters so I wouldn't know what was going on! Were you *trying* to break Todd and me up?"

"How can you say that?" Jessica cried. "You and Todd are the perfect couple! I thought he'd just be flattered by the first letter you wrote for that girl. I didn't think any harm would come from some silly crush."

"Silly crush!" Elizabeth shrieked. "You let me help this . . . this *girl* steal my boyfriend!"

"It's your fault, too, Elizabeth," Jessica said quickly. "If you hadn't written a letter full of such romantic nonsense in the first place, none of this would have happened. I tried to get you to tone it down, remember?"

"Lousy excuse, Jess," Elizabeth said, glaring at her sister. "If you had told me in the first place what was going on, I never would have *written* that letter, not one word of it. I would have gone directly to this girl and confronted her on the spot."

"But you couldn't have done that, Liz. Our service is supposed to be confidential," Jessica retorted. "And how was I supposed to know that Todd would take her up on her offer? I can't read people's minds."

"It's a good thing you can't read mine right now," Elizabeth shouted.

"I *tried* to get the letters back from the mailman, Liz. I was going to rewrite them and discourage both Todd and the girl from seeing each other," Jessica explained. "I waited for half an hour at Todd's house to intercept Mr. Ramsey, but when I did catch up with him he wouldn't give me the envelope. He said it was against the law—"

"I don't want to hear it!" Elizabeth stood up and slammed the empty pitcher down on the table. "All I want to know is the name of the girl."

"Now, Elizabeth," Jessica said, quickly wiping up the drops of juice that had spattered on the surface. "You're not yourself. I mean, the cake, the juice, your books in the hall . . . don't you think you should calm down a bit before you talk to her?"

Elizabeth smiled and sat down. She folded her hands in front of her on the table. "I *am* calm," she said, leaning forward intently. "But I won't be much longer if you don't tell me her name. Besides, I'm not going to talk to *her*. I'm going to talk to Todd." She slammed her fist onto the table. "Now who is she?"

Jessica slumped back in her chair. "It's Shelley. Shelley Novak," she said quietly.

"Thank you," Elizabeth said. Then she got up from her seat, spun around, and stormed out of the kitchen.

Thirteen

Elizabeth drove straight over to Todd's house. She knew he would be home. Basketball practice should have finished over an hour ago. A sudden pang of jealousy hit her. Unless he was out with Shelley, of course.

She rang the doorbell.

Todd answered. "Elizabeth?"

"You weren't expecting to see me, were you?" she asked angrily as she marched past him into his house. "What's the meaning of *this?*" She waved the letter in his face. "Is this all I'm worth to you? A Dear Jane form letter?"

Elizabeth noted that Todd at least had the decency to look uncomfortable. But looking uncomfortable didn't solve anything.

"Well?" Elizabeth demanded. "Why do you want to go out with someone else?"

"I didn't want to, but you gave me no choice," Todd replied defensively.

"No choice?" Elizabeth cried. "I'm a little busy, so you cut me off without a clue? I thought we had something special."

"We do," Todd said. "We did."

Elizabeth folded her arms. "Did?"

She could see that Todd was getting angry now, too. He ran his hands through his hair. *Good*, she thought. *Let's have it out right now!*

"Look, Elizabeth," he began. "*You're* the one who's been ignoring *me*. What's a guy supposed to do when his girlfriend doesn't have time for him anymore?"

"Trade her in for a new model, I guess," Elizabeth shot back. "How *dare* you suggest that I went to the concert with someone else, when all along *you* were dating someone behind my back?"

"I haven't started dating her. Yet!" Todd shouted.

"And what am I supposed to do now? Come crawling back to you and beg you not to dump me? Forget it. I have better things to do."

"Obviously," Todd said, his voice dripping with sarcasm. "Every time I've called you or asked you out during the past few weeks, you've had something *better* to do."

"It wasn't like that at all!" Elizabeth cried.

"What was it like then, Elizabeth, huh? What *is* this big project you and Jessica have been working on? And how could it possibly have anything to do with me?"

"I wouldn't tell you now if the world were going to fall apart in thirty seconds," Elizabeth told him. "You don't have, never have had, and never *will* have the right to demand to know what I do with my time. We're not joined at the hip, you know!"

"What a way to put it," Todd said hoarsely. "But then, lately we're not joined in anything!"

"Shows how much you know," Elizabeth retorted. She thought about how connected with him she had felt the whole time she was earning money to buy him the warmup jacket. But it had all been a waste of time, a sham. Todd didn't trust her. As soon as she started spending time away from him, he immediately thought the worst.

"I don't know anything. That's my problem," Todd countered.

Elizabeth rolled her eyes. They were getting nowhere with this stupid argument. She was tired and angry and hurt. She had to get out of here.

"Well, maybe your new *girlfriend* can enlighten you," she said.

She flung open the front door and walked with her head held high to her Jeep. She got in and gunned the engine. She was proud of herself for not having mentioned Shelley's name. Then Todd would have known that she had written the letters. And that was something she did *not* want him to know.

Let him stew, she thought. *Let him go out with Shelley this weekend.* But if he thought that Shelley was capable of writing a love letter like the one Elizabeth had written for her, then he was sadly mistaken. He had a surprise in store for him, that was for sure. There was only one Elizabeth Wakefield—and he had been stupid enough to lose her!

Elizabeth drove a few blocks, fueled by dignity and pride. And then she pulled over to the side of the road and burst into tears.

Shelley waited by the discreet wooden sign outside the Box Tree Café, the place where she and Todd had agreed to meet for their dinner date. She squeezed her hands together to stop them from shaking and thought about the day that she had received Todd's romantic letter.

She had arrived home from basketball practice Monday, to be greeted at the door by her mother.

"Going out, Mom?" Shelley had asked.

"I have to run to the grocery store. I've been so busy around here all day that I haven't had the time to shop. Is there anything special you want for dinner?"

Shelley had smiled. "Whatever you get will be fine," she had said.

"There's a letter for you in the mail basket on the kitchen counter. And a message from Jim pinned to the bulletin board," her mother had told her. "I'll see you in a little while."

Shelley had barely managed to say goodbye. *Who would be sending me a letter except . . . Todd?* she had thought. She had dropped her books on the sofa and hurried to the kitchen. Then she had stood there, the letter from Todd in one hand, the message from Jim in the other. The message said that Jim wanted her to call him. The letter was a mystery, waiting to be solved. She had wavered, trying to decide which to do first, open the letter or call Jim.

She had called Jim.

"Hey, Shel," he had said as soon as he recognized her voice. "How ya doin'?"

"OK, I guess," Shelley remembered saying while the letter from Todd burned an imaginary hole in her hand. "How about you?"

"Not so good, actually," Jim had said. "I know we were supposed to get together tonight, and I hate to cancel out on you again, but my parents have to go out tonight and they want me to watch my little brother."

"I could come over and help you," Shelley had offered. "I'm a good babysitter."

"I know you are, but my parents won't let me have friends over when I'm babysitting. I've told you that, haven't I? It's a major rule around here. I'm sorry. I hope you understand."

"Sure, no problem," Shelley had said as she fiddled with the flap on the letter. "Some other time."

"You can bet on it," Jim had said, and his enthusiasm had almost made her feel guilty for wanting him to get off the phone so that she could read Todd's letter. Almost, but not quite.

"Well, I'll see you in school tomorrow," she had said.

"Yeah, tomorrow," Jim had echoed.

The second she had hung up the phone, she had torn open Todd's letter. The letter inside was typed, but then so was the one she had sent him.

Dear Shelley, it had read. *I really loved your letter. It was the best letter I've ever received. Up until now, I never realized that you felt this way about me . . . Will you go out with me on Friday night? I'd like to have the chance to get to know you better . . .* Todd's signature was a flourish across the bottom of the page.

"Oh, no!" Shelley had exclaimed. "I never expected *this!*"

Shelley had never really believed that Todd would be interested in her. In a romantic way, that is. All along she had assumed he would tell her that being friends was great, but that there couldn't be any more to their relationship. In fact, she had been so convinced that Todd would turn her down that she hadn't given much thought to what she would do if he *did* ask her out. And once he had, suddenly Shelley hadn't been so sure she wanted to accept his offer.

If the truth were known, she had come to realize that her romantic feelings for Todd were mostly a result of her frustration over Jim, and had very little to do with Todd himself. In the last few days she had come to admit to herself that she had been *counting* on Todd to turn her down. And she had been so sure he would. He and Elizabeth were so tight!

But maybe they weren't so tight after all. Shelley had glanced at the phone and thought about Jim. How many times had she seen him during the past couple of weeks, except for at school and in passing? Once? Twice? She deserved more than that from her boyfriend.

Well, I've gone this far, she had thought. *I might as well go further.* She had picked up the phone and punched in Todd's number. She hadn't allowed herself time to think or reconsider. If she had, she might not be standing outside of a restaurant, twisting her hands and taking deep, cleansing breaths.

This is much worse than the last five minutes of a tied game, Shelley told herself. Oh, why had she called Todd to say she would come? She had never felt more uncomfortable in her life. She looked down at her soft black skirt and silky jade-green blouse. She had spent hours getting ready to meet with Todd. It had been strange. She had never worried about what she looked like for Todd before! But this wasn't like any of the other times they'd spent together in the past. This was different—and it was scary.

Just remember what you're here for, Shelley said to herself soothingly. *You're not here to start a relationship. You're here to end one.*

"Shelley!" Todd called as he came into view. He walked quickly up to her, and Shelley felt about two zillion nerve endings snap.

"I'm glad we decided to meet outside," Todd said with a smile that to Shelley seemed only slightly strained. "I hate standing in front of a crowded room where everyone can watch me while I search for someone."

"You sound experienced at that sort of thing," Shelley commented nervously.

"It only happened to me once. That was enough. C'mon. Let's go inside."

Actually, Shelley decided, Todd didn't seem shy or uncomfortable at all. He led her inside and secured them a table as if he had been dating people other than Elizabeth for years. When he held her chair out for her and his hand touched her shoulder, she almost bolted.

Why did I come? Why did I send the letter? What will Elizabeth think of me? Shelley fretted.

"I'm uh . . . glad you came," Todd said suddenly.

"Me, too," Shelley said, gulping as she smiled shyly into his dark brown eyes. *But not for the same reason,* she thought.

"So, have you been here before?"

"Once, with Jim."

"Oh." There was a long silence. "They have good food, don't they?"

"Yes," Shelley answered while she searched her brain for something else to say. "Have you?"

"Have I what?"

"Been here before?"

"Oh, sure. I come here with my parents a lot. They like the flounder Florentine."

"I kind of like chicken better," Shelley said. Somehow talking to Todd on a date and talking to Todd as a friend were two totally different things. She had been right when she'd realized her romantic impulses toward Todd were only the result of her feeling neglected by Jim. No doubt about it—she definitely liked being his friend more than she liked being his date.

Todd smiled and opened his menu. "I like chicken better, too," he said, looking up briefly and then returning his eyes to the menu. "I guess that means we have two things in common—basketball and chicken."

And cheesecake and slapstick, Shelley thought. *But not romance*.

Shelley looked at the top of Todd's bowed head and knew she couldn't keep up the pretense for another minute. It was Jim she loved. Jim, with all of his faults and his obsession with his work and his tendency to be off in his own little world filled with developing solutions and light-meter readings. She had come on the date to clear up the mess she had gotten them both into by sending that first letter, and that was what she was going to do.

"Todd, could we talk seriously for a moment?" Shelley asked.

"We've always been able to talk, Shelley," Todd said. "That's one of the things I like about you. You're a good listener."

"So are you," Shelley told him. "And I've really appreciated having you as my sounding board on more than one occasion."

"Happy to oblige," Todd said, grinning crookedly and tipping an imaginary hat. "Shelley, I have to tell you that your letter was so wonderful. I think it was the best letter I've ever received."

"I loved your letter, too," Shelley said truthfully. "It made me feel so . . . special, like someone really cared enough to take the time to write. Jim hasn't had much time for me lately."

"Nor Elizabeth for me," Todd admitted.

"That's probably what got us into this mess in the first place," Shelley mumbled.

"I'm sorry. I didn't catch that," Todd said.

Shelley closed her eyes for a second, opened them, and plunged ahead. "I have something to confess," she told him. "I feel really nervous and kind of uncomfortable being here with you. I don't know what to say now that we're actually on a date."

Todd ran a finger under his collar. Then he laughed softly. "I'm glad to hear you say that. I thought *I* was the only one feeling a bit awkward."

"You've got to be kidding," Shelley teased. "Anyone would think you were an old pro at this."

"Not quite. I'm sure old pros don't sweat so much that their shirt sticks to the back of the seat."

Todd's honesty made Shelley feel better immediately. It made it easier for her to tell him the rest of what she had to say. "I may as well confess all," she added. "I didn't write that letter I sent you. I hired that new letter-writing service, Letters R Us, to do it for me."

"You did?" Todd said. "You're not going to believe this, but so did I."

"You're kidding!"

"Nope. Your letter was so great that I wanted to make sure mine was as good as yours. I knew I needed professional help for that, so I hired the service."

Shelley grinned. "Well, while we're on this honesty kick," she said, "I have to tell you something else."

"There's more?" Todd asked.

Shelley nodded. "I never read the letter I sent you. I started feeling so guilty about it that I just signed my name and stuck it in the mail the way it was."

Todd laughed heartily. "I can't believe it! What a coincidence! I didn't read the letter *I* sent *you*, either. I just put your name on the top, signed my name on the bottom, and sent it."

In unison, they both leaned across the table and said, "So what did the letter say?"

"I have it right here," they both answered. And then they coughed identically nervous coughs.

Shelley reached in her purse, and Todd dug in his back pocket. Slowly they exchanged the letters.

"Oh, my!" Shelley exclaimed after she had read the first paragraph.

"I don't believe this!" Todd said.

"I can't—"

Suddenly, the whole thing was too much for Shelley. She started giggling, and then her giggles turned to all-out laughter. Todd joined her, and when the waiter came to take their order they were laughing so hard that he just poured them two glasses of water and left in a huff.

Finally, Shelley wiped her eyes on her napkin. "I take it that you didn't mean to say those things?" she asked.

"Well," Todd began, "I thought it would be nice to go out with you. That much is true. And you *are* a good friend."

"I consider you a good friend, too, Todd," Shelley said. "But I've been doing a lot of thinking these past couple of days and I realized that I value our friendship too much to jeopardize it by trying to turn it into something else. Besides, I really love Jim," she added.

"And I really love Elizabeth," Todd said softly.

"I didn't know how to tell you," Shelley went on. "After reading your letter I thought you'd be mad at me for leading you on. I don't know what got into me, Todd. Jim has been so busy lately, and I was feeling neglected, I guess. You were so kind to me, and I suppose I wished that Jim was more like you."

"I'm flattered," Todd said. "Elizabeth has been giving me the busy routine lately, too," he added. "I guess I wanted to feel cared about again, and your letter came at just the right time."

"Boy, talk about missing the rebound," Shelley said. "I take it this means that we don't have to worry about being romantic anymore?"

"Right. Friends?" Todd asked, sticking his hand across the table.

Shelley shook it firmly. "Friends."

This time when the waiter approached their table, they managed to order without incident. For the rest of the evening they ate and talked and enjoyed each other's company.

"There's still one thing I want to know,

though," Todd said when their dinner plates had been taken away and they were waiting for dessert. "Who's behind the letter-writing service?"

"I don't know," Shelley said with a shrug. "Someone out there knows our secrets. I don't mind making a fool of myself in private, but I don't want the whole school—or maybe even the whole town—to be in on it."

"I think I may have a plan," Todd said, lowering his voice dramatically.

Shelley giggled and pretended to check under the table for bugging devices.

"Since the service's posters are up all over Sweet Valley High, I'm going to make the wild guess that the people behind the service are students," Todd whispered.

"A valid supposition," Shelley whispered back.

"And chances are they pick up their mail in the afternoons when school lets out. If I stake out the post office for a few days, maybe I can catch them," Todd said.

"I'll help," Shelley offered. "I could watch the post office in the mornings. And when we do find out who is behind the service, we'll make *sure* they know we want this matter kept completely confidential!"

Fourteen

Jessica hummed as she walked into the post office on Saturday afternoon. It wouldn't be long, if things kept going the way they were, before Letters R Us could close its doors forever. *Or maybe we'll sell the business,* Jessica thought. It would be a quick and easy way to make some extra money on the way out.

She didn't notice Todd sneaking up behind her until it was too late.

"Aha!" Todd said accusingly. "Why didn't I suspect it from the first?"

"Suspect what, Todd?" Jessica cried as she tried to hide the key behind her back.

"You know *what*," Todd said. "You were behind the letter-writing business all along!" Todd leaned back against the wall of numbered boxes. "I want the entire truth now."

"OK, I'm caught," Jessica admitted. "Actually,

I'm glad it's finally over, that you finally know the truth. But you're wrong about one thing," she said. "I'm not the one actually *writing* the letters. Elizabeth writes them. I just pick up, deliver, and sort. And do our books."

"Elizabeth writes the letters?" Todd asked. "I don't believe it! I don't understand it! Why would she write a romantic letter to Shelley and a rejection letter to herself? And then get furious at me for sending it to her? Unless . . ." Todd was silent for a moment, his expression sad. "Unless she really *did* want me to fall for Shelley because she *wanted* to break up in the first place."

Jessica patted Todd's shoulder. She knew she was going to have to tell him the whole story. Perhaps if she leveled with Todd she could extricate herself, and them all, from this horrible mess.

Jessica took the stack of requests from the post office box, then closed and locked it. "Walk me to my car, Todd. I'll be happy to tell you everything."

"It's about time someone did," Todd said miserably.

"Look," Jessica told him, "Elizabeth *doesn't* want to break up with you. In fact, just the opposite is true. We started the letter-writing service because I wanted to make some money to buy a CD player for the Jeep, a dress, and racing gloves for Sam. And Elizabeth did it because she wanted to buy a present for you!"

Todd's jaw dropped. "Then why the letters? Why didn't she say something to me the minute she saw the letter from Shelley?"

Jessica turned her head and tried to gather her thoughts. Then she turned back to Todd. He had the right to hear every sordid detail. "She never knew the letter was from Shelley or that it was going to you," she explained. "I rewrote the letters before she saw them, changed the names, that sort of thing. When she wrote that letter for Shelley, she thought she was helping some girl named Blythe from a different high school."

"But Jess, why? Why didn't you just—"

Jessica held up her hands. "*Please*, Todd, don't. I've asked myself the same question about a million times. The point is, I let her write those love letters—"

"No wonder I loved Shelley's letter so much," Todd said, interrupting Jessica's speech. "Liz wrote it! And then I made her write those letters to Shelley and to herself . . . I feel so dumb!"

"I tried to stop her from sending those letters to you," Jessica told him. "And I went to great lengths, as a matter of fact, to get the letters back, but the mailman was bigger than me."

"Very funny," Todd said ruefully.

"You didn't have to send them," Jessica countered. "You could have trusted Elizabeth in the first place. She's very hurt, you know."

"I know she's hurt. She came over to my house and blew up at me. I haven't talked to her since. I was so mad at her because she wouldn't tell me what she was up to that I kept my date with Shelley last night."

"And?" Jessica prodded. "What about it? What happened?"

Todd smiled. "Shelley and I are just friends. It didn't take us long to realize that it had all been a big misunderstanding. I think she's over at Jim's house talking to him right now."

"Well, that's a relief," Jessica said with a sigh. "But what are you going to do about Elizabeth?"

Todd straightened his shoulders. "Hey, I'll be the first to admit I've been an idiot about this whole thing. I'm going to talk to her today, and I hope we can work things out."

"Good," Jessica said as she got in and started the Jeep. "I suppose I'll be seeing you later," she called as she drove off, a smile tugging at her lips. *Thank goodness that's settled*, she thought.

Unfortunately, Jessica could not convince her sister that everything was settled. Against Jessica's repeated advice, Elizabeth refused to take Todd's phone calls that afternoon and evening and refused to see him when he showed up three times on Sunday.

Shelley knew that she was going to have to be the one to put her relationship with Jim back on track. *Of course*, Shelley thought as she rang Jim's bell on Saturday, *Jim doesn't even know that anything was wrong!* She knew that their communication problem was as much hers as it was his.

"Hi, Shel," Jim greeted her when he answered the door. "C'mon in. I want to show you something."

Shelley followed Jim into his living room, where he had the photos for the yearbook, complete with their captions, spread out all over the floor.

"How do you like this one of you?" he asked, showing her an action shot in which she was dribbling in front of several guards from another team. Her expression was determined, her eye on the basket.

"And these?" Jim directed her attention to the second and third pictures in the series.

Shelley laughed as she saw he had captured the entire play in sequence. The second one was of her leaping high in front of the surprised defense. Jim had captured the ball in midair, heading for the basket. The third photograph showed the winning shot, the ball on its way through the net. In the foreground of the picture Shelley and her teammates were airborne, jumping for joy.

"I'm really impressed," Shelley told him. "You must have had that shutter clicking a mile a minute."

"Yep," Jim said proudly. "But sometimes even I can't keep up with you." He leaned over and kissed her gently. "Thanks for putting up with me while I buried myself in my work for the past few weeks. I've really missed you."

"I've missed you, too," Shelley said, kissing him back. It felt so good to be with him, to hear him say that he had missed her. It would be so easy, she decided, just to ignore what had happened. Jim didn't need to know that she had almost dropped him for Todd Wilkins. He didn't need to know about the letters or the date, or about her sleepless nights wondering whether he still cared for her. She looked into his trusting eyes.

Then again, maybe he did.

"Jim, can we talk a bit?" Shelley said tentatively. "I want to tell you a story about what's been happening to me while you've been so busy."

"Sure, Shel. Is there a problem?"

"Sort of," Shelley admitted. "I think the problem is communication. Or the lack of it. I guess I was feeling neglected and just didn't know how to tell you. Instead of talking about it with you, I—I complained about you to Todd. He was very kind to me, and for a while I thought that maybe I was falling for him."

"Todd?" Jim's face clearly showed his hurt. "While I've been working in the darkroom, you've been falling for another guy?"

"Not exactly," Shelley said. She smiled and reached for Jim's hand. "Todd and I are *just friends*. What makes him such a good friend is that I can tell him anything and he listens. I used to feel that way about you. When we first started going out, we talked all the time. Lately, though, we seem to have run out of things to talk about. We're kind of in a rut."

Jim smiled ruefully. "I've noticed that, too. Maybe that's why I've spent so much time lately working on photography projects for *The Oracle* and the yearbook. I sort of thought you were getting tired of me."

"You thought I was getting tired of you?" Shelley exclaimed. "I thought *you* were getting tired of *me!*"

"No way," Jim told her. "I love you, Shelley. We just don't seem to have that much in common. I mean, we took that ballroom-dancing class together, but we haven't been dancing since. I like to go to your games and practices, but frankly, I've been wondering what we'll do after you've won the state championship."

"Well, thanks for the vote of confidence," Shelley said.

"In my mind there's no doubt about the outcome," Jim answered. "I'm saving a spot in the yearbook for the photo that shows you winning. But back to the subject. I've never been much good at coming up with fun things to do. I'm kind of a boring guy."

"Join the crowd," Shelley said with a grin. "We're both so intense about one thing only that neither of us has branched out much." Shelley smiled. "I know! Let's brainstorm some ideas for things we can do together, things that have nothing to do with basketball or photography."

"Sweet Valley *does* have a lot to offer." Jim frowned. "But I don't know, Shelley. I'm usually a spectator."

"Me, too. Until we got together, I was too ashamed of my height to do anything in public but play basketball!"

"I'm glad you're over *that*. I don't know what I'd do if I had a girlfriend so short that I had to bend down to kiss her." Jim demonstrated how well they fit together by pulling her into his arms and kissing her then and there.

"You'd probably have a bad back," Shelley teased. "I'm glad I've saved you from that particular fate. We can be boring but healthy together."

"I have an idea," Jim said suddenly. "How about miniature golf? Have you ever played?"

Shelley shook her head.

"Neither have I. We can look stupid together." Jim reached for a sheet of paper. "I'm going to make a list right now," he said.

"I think we should go dancing some more. I hear a new teen rock club is opening up in town. Under eighteen only."

"Sounds great," Jim said excitedly as he added the idea to their list. "I think we're on a roll here," he added. "How about water skiing?"

"Uh-huh. What about hiking? I love to walk."

"Bike riding? Picnicking? Scuba diving?"

Shelley laughed. "I don't think we'll be running out of things to do for a while."

"Or things to talk about," Jim added.

"Listen, let's not let this happen again," Shelley said, suddenly serious. "It's scary to think that we might have broken up just because we didn't *talk* to each other."

"It's even scarier to think that I might not have noticed because I was hiding out with my work," Jim said. "I promise I won't ever let that happen again."

"And I promise that if you don't retreat, I'll talk to *you* about any problems before I talk to other people," Shelley told him. "I've learned that being direct is best. It's just like driving for the basket. Sometimes you have to plow through the defensive line, take aim, and shoot before anyone has a chance to distract you."

Jim put his arm around her and drew her close. He grinned and pointed to his lips. "I'd like you to direct a kiss right here," he teased. "Just plow through all of my defenses."

"Clear a path!" she teased.

"Go for it, Novak!" Jim cheered. "Aim and shoot!"

And she did.

Fifteen

"No problem, Olivia," Elizabeth assured her friend and fellow reporter as she opened the door to leave the *Oracle* office on Monday.

"I really appreciate your taking on an extra article so close to deadline," Olivia told her. "This article I've been writing on school vandalism is turning into more than I expected. Every time I discover one piece of damage, someone tells me about another."

"That's happened to me before, too," Elizabeth said. "I'm happy to help. Besides, suddenly I find that I have extra time on my hands."

Too much time, Elizabeth thought sadly as she left the office. Without Todd, her life seemed emptier. She was going to have to take on all kinds of extra jobs to fill up her days so that she wouldn't have to imagine him spending time with Shelley.

"Liz?" a voice said tentatively the moment she stepped out into the hallway. "I'd like to talk to you."

Elizabeth looked at Todd. She knew her sadness showed in her eyes. He was so dear to her, and she still loved him so much. She didn't know how she could stand to watch Todd and Shelley become a couple after she and Todd had meant so much to each other. This was even worse than when Todd had moved to Vermont. At least then she had known the separation wasn't his choice.

"I don't see what there is left to talk about," Elizabeth said softly, turning away and continuing down the hall.

"I think there's a *lot* to talk about," Todd went on, following her. "Shelley and I went out the other night and we realized—"

"I don't want to hear about it, Todd," Elizabeth interrupted. *Please don't tell me about your date,* she begged silently.

"But you don't know what I'm going to say, Todd protested.

"If you have anything to say, you'd better say it to Shelley. I don't want to be just friends, Todd."

Elizabeth quickened her pace. She had to get away from him. She was positive that he was going to tell her how well he and Shelley had hit it off and what a good sport Elizabeth was being about the whole thing. But she *wasn't* being a good sport. She *hated* the thought that Todd was dating another girl.

"You don't understand!" Todd cried as he caught up with her.

"I understand a lot of things," Elizabeth replied. "You were feeling neglected and I was busy, so you found someone else. I'm tired of playing games, Todd. Either you have me or you have Shelley, but you can't have us both!"

Elizabeth pushed open the big double doors of the school and jogged down the steps. She headed for the parking lot, aware that Todd had stopped at the top of the stairs. She tried not to, but couldn't help taking just one glance back to where he was still standing, watching her.

Tears in her eyes, Elizabeth got into the Jeep, started the motor, and drove away.

If only Todd had told her he was feeling neglected earlier on! But maybe he had, and it was her fault for not listening closely enough. Oh, if only Jessica had told her the truth about the letters! But then again, why hadn't she herself been sensitive enough to read between the lines, to realize that Todd had been describing her own behavior, to see that the wonderful boy Shelley had been describing was Todd? Instead, she had focused only on the project, on doing the work fast and well, and on her intention of buying Todd the jacket. Now it was too late—for her relationship and for the stupid jacket.

Elizabeth parked the car in the garage, hardly aware of the fact that she had actually driven home. As she walked up to the front door she saw the package. Her vision blurred by tears, she read the line on the mailing label: *Your U.S. Sports order has arrived.*

Slowly, Elizabeth picked up the box and entered the house. And in her head, her own thoughts echoed: *Too late. Too late. Too late.*

Jessica wasn't completely surprised to find Todd waiting for her outside the gym after cheerleading practice. She knew how stubborn her twin could be. She knew that Elizabeth had refused Todd's calls and visits all weekend, but she had been hoping that when Todd caught her sister in person at school, they would finally be able to talk things out. Obviously, she had been wrong.

"She wouldn't talk to you, huh?" Jessica asked, falling into step with Todd.

"She won't listen to a word I say. I tried to tell her that Shelley and I are just friends and that I love *her*, but she just ran away."

"So I suppose you want me to talk to her," Jessica said. "But to tell you the truth, Todd, I doubt she'll listen to me, either. At least not if I try to talk about you."

"Well, I've been thinking about it, and I've come up with a plan that might get me through to her," Todd said. "Will you help me?"

Elizabeth was trying, but not succeeding, to concentrate on her homework when Jessica knocked on her door.

"Are you still speaking to me?" Jessica asked.

"Of course I am," Elizabeth said, smiling lightly. "I can never be mad at you for long, Jess."

"I just wanted to tell you again how sorry I am about the way things worked out."

"That's OK, Jess. It's not your fault that Todd

147

went out with Shelley," Elizabeth said. "If anyone is to blame, it's me. I'm the one who was so wrapped up in her work that she didn't notice her boyfriend needed her. And I'm the one who wrote those stupid romantic letters."

"Oh, skip the poor-me routine," Jessica said fervently. "You know that you still love Todd and that he loves you. Right now the two of you are having a communication problem, but it will pass. Trust your little sister, Liz."

"I wish I could believe you," Elizabeth said a bit ruefully. "I *do* still love Todd, in spite of the fact that he doesn't want to be with me anymore. When his jacket came in the mail today, I cried all over it."

Jessica put her arms around her sister. "It's going to be OK. I know it will," she said encouragingly.

"In time, maybe," Elizabeth replied, hugging her sister tightly before sitting back down. "In time I suppose I'll find someone else and get used to seeing Todd and Shelley walk around school together," she added. "But right now I feel pretty rotten. In fact, I might as well distract myself with work. Where are the requests that you picked up at the post office today?"

Jessica dug in her backpack and pulled out that day's stack of mail. "Listen, I figured you probably wouldn't be up to answering letters today, so I took the liberty of writing the responses. There were only a few."

"You really do know how to read my mind, Jess," Elizabeth said. "I guess I'm really *not* up to

148

helping other people with their problems right now. I have enough of my own."

"Unfortunately," Jessica said, pulling one envelope out of the stack, "there was *one* that I had trouble with, and I was hoping that you could help me for just a few minutes. Then I promise I'll leave you alone."

"OK. Let me see it."

Elizabeth took the neatly folded letter and opened it. The minute she saw the handwriting, she knew it was from Todd. Her hand shook and tears threatened again. "I can't do it, Jess. I can't write another love letter for him to send to Shelley."

"Here, let me read it to you," Jessica said, reaching for the letter. She cleared her throat. "Dear Letters R Us, I really love my girlfriend, but I've made a big mess out of our relationship. I assumed she wasn't interested in me anymore, but I found out that she was working the whole time to buy me a nice present. I went out with another girl in between, but realized immediately that we can only be friends. I know I was wrong not to talk to my girlfriend about my feelings. Now she won't give me a chance to explain, and I don't know what to do."

Elizabeth was crying now, but Jessica relentlessly read on. "Can you please write a letter apologizing for me? I love her so much that I can't stand the thought of being without her."

Jessica looked up from the letter. "What do you know? It's signed Todd Wilkins."

For several long moments, Elizabeth cried silently

on Jessica's shoulder. "So it was all just a big mis-understanding?" Elizabeth said, sniffling. "Todd and Shelley *aren't* together? He still loves me?"

"Of course he does," Jessica assured her.

Elizabeth took the letter out of Jessica's hand. "I guess I should be the one to write back to him. But I don't know what to say."

Jessica stood up and headed for the door. "Just tell him how you feel," she suggested.

As soon as Jessica was gone Elizabeth sat down at her computer to write. At first she just stared at the blank blue screen. Then words, unbidden and heartfelt, sprang to her fingertips.

Dear Todd,

Your letter meant more to me than I can say. It's obvious that even a person like me, who lives with words every day, sometimes has trouble saying what she means. It was wrong of me not to tell you the truth about what I was doing. So what if it would have spoiled your surprise? Our relationship should have meant more to me than my pride. I guess I just didn't realize how much I was shutting you out. I'm sorry. Please forgive me. I can't stand the thought of being without you, either.

Love, Liz.

Elizabeth sealed the envelope and wrote Todd's name on the front. Lovingly, she wrapped his new jacket in tissue paper and tied it with a satin ribbon. She picked up the letter and package and went into the bathroom she shared with Jessica to splash cold water on her face. Then she raised her head for a quick glance in the mirror.

Elizabeth smiled at her reflection, the first genuine smile, it seemed, that she had smiled in days.

"Where are you off to?" Jessica asked as she met Elizabeth in the hall outside their rooms. She eyed the package and the envelope. "Don't you want to stay and help me paint?" she asked, holding up a roller and a tray. "I've already cleared the floor and covered the furniture."

Elizabeth gave Jessica a quick sideways hug with her free arm. "I'll help you some other time. I finished writing Todd's letter," she told her. "But I can't wait for tomorrow's mail. This is one letter I'm going to deliver myself!"

"Good luck," Jessica called after her as Elizabeth ran down the stairs.

Elizabeth didn't even have to look back up. She knew Jessica was grinning.

The drive to Todd's house had never seemed so beautiful. Each palm-lined street in the exclusive neighborhood seemed to beckon her onward, welcoming her. She relished the caressing warmth of the ocean breeze and the clear azure blue of the sky. She touched the package, letting the cool, satiny ribbon slip through her fingers. Everything was going to be all right. She could feel it.

But when she arrived and parked the Jeep in front of Todd's house, she suddenly felt nervous. She wasn't sure she wanted to talk to him just yet. Maybe she would wait to see his reaction to the letter and package before she made her presence known.

Fate, however, intervened. Just as Elizabeth was laying the package on the steps of the Wilkinses' home and pushing the letter through the mail slot, Todd opened the door.

"I, uh, just wanted to deliver these," Elizabeth said quickly. She started to back down the steps.

Todd looked down at the letter and the package at his feet. "Please don't go, Liz," he asked gently.

Elizabeth bit her bottom lip but didn't retreat any further. As Todd opened her letter she closed her eyes.

There were a few minutes of interminable silence as Todd read what she had written. She knew the letter by heart and she mentally followed along with him.

When she opened her eyes, Todd was standing only inches from her. He took her in his arms, and she laid her head on his chest.

"I love you, Elizabeth," Todd whispered into her hair. "I'm so sorry for doubting you."

Elizabeth looked up at him, happiness shining in her eyes. "I love you, too," she said. "I'm sorry that you thought I had stopped."

They kissed then, treasuring the new trust that bloomed like a flower between them.

"You know about the letter-writing service, don't you?" Elizabeth asked when they finally released each other.

Todd nodded. "I caught Jessica at the post office and she confessed everything. I wish you had told me earlier, but I can understand why you wanted to keep your identities a secret."

"It wasn't so much that I didn't want you to know about the service," Elizabeth explained. "But I know how clever you are, and I figured you'd find out that I was working to buy you this." She reached down and handed Todd the package. "I hope you like it."

"If it's from you, I'll love it," Todd said, swooping in for another kiss before he untied the ribbons. A moment later he was holding up the jacket in amazement. "Wow! This is perfect!"

"I knew you needed one, and when I saw this one in the U.S. Sports catalog, I couldn't resist," Elizabeth told him. "Try it on."

"First I want to try it on you," Todd said, wrapping the silky material around Elizabeth and helping her slide her arms into it.

"Why am I trying it on?" Elizabeth asked, snuggling against him as he hugged her tightly.

"Because I wouldn't think of wearing this—"

"What?" Elizabeth gasped, pushing away from him.

"You didn't let me finish," Todd said, chucking her playfully under the chin. "You have a habit of that lately."

"Sorry," Elizabeth said, folding her arms across her chest and letting the sleeves dangle. "You were saying . . . ?"

Todd grinned. "I was saying that I wouldn't think of wearing this unless you let me order a matching one for you. After all, I want everyone

153

to know we're meant for each other, now and for all time."

When Elizabeth and Todd walked into the *Oracle* office a week later wearing matching blue-and-gold warmup jackets, they caused quite a stir.

"Nice," Penny Ayala, *The Oracle's* editor-in-chief, complimented them. "Hey, Olivia. Come out here. You have to see this."

Olivia strolled out from the back room, where she and her boyfriend, Rod Sullivan, were laying out the artwork for the paper. "You're liable to start a new fad," Olivia said, grinning. "All the couples at Sweet Valley High will want to wear matching jackets. We'll have to run a feature article on it in the paper."

"Of course, what would happen if the couple broke up?" Penny speculated. "What a waste of a good jacket!"

"On the other hand," Rod said, emerging with a sheet of layouts to proof, "what if you and your girlfriend don't look good in the same colors? I mean, this could really cause a scandal. The whole fabric of the school could fall apart."

"All right, that's enough!" Todd said, chuckling good-naturedly.

"That's right," Elizabeth put in. "Don't you guys have anything more interesting to talk about than the spring fashion preview?"

"How about interior design?" Olivia asked. "I interviewed Jessica and the cheerleading squad yesterday, and all she could talk about was her new purple room."

"Jessica has gone purple crazy, that's for sure," Elizabeth agreed. "It only took her a week, but now she has purple walls, a purple ceiling, purple pillows, and a purple rug. Her room looks like a grape explosion."

"I don't know how you can stand it," Olivia commented.

Elizabeth laughed. "Jessica wouldn't be Jessica if she didn't go to extremes. Hey, Penny, speaking of outstanding behavior, Mr. Collins told me about that two-week Government in Action program you applied for."

"Just think of the articles I'll be able to write after I've been following a senator around for two weeks," Penny said dreamily. "But I'm trying not to get my hopes up," she added quickly. "I won't know for sure if I've been chosen until later in the week."

"What's the final choice based on?" Olivia asked.

"A paper that I wrote entitled, 'How I Would Change Politics in the United States,' " Penny told them.

"You shouldn't have any trouble, Penny," Elizabeth assured her. "You're one of the best writers around. You'd better start packing. Washington, D.C., here she comes!"

"But what's going to happen to the paper while you're gone?" Olivia asked. "We have the big teacher exposé issue coming up, and the Sports Report insert . . ."

Penny shook her head. "In all the excitement I almost forgot. But I'm sure Mr. Collins can find someone to take over for me while I'm gone."

Who will be chosen to be editor-in-chief of The Oracle *in Penny's absence? Find out in Sweet Valley High #89,* **ELIZABETH BETRAYED.**